Love, Lilly

LOVE ALWAYS BOOK ONE

Love, Lilly

BELINDA MARY

H&J Publishing

Copyright © 2023 by Belinda Mary

All rights reserved.

The story, all names, characters, and incidents portrayed in this production are fictitious. No identification with actual persons (living or deceased), places, buildings, and products is intended or should be inferred.

Cover Illustrations by Lorissa Padilla Designs

1st edition 2023

ISBN: 978-0-6456942-1-5

www.belindamary.com

To Philip, Hunter, Sienna and Rocky.
You are my everything.

CONTENTS

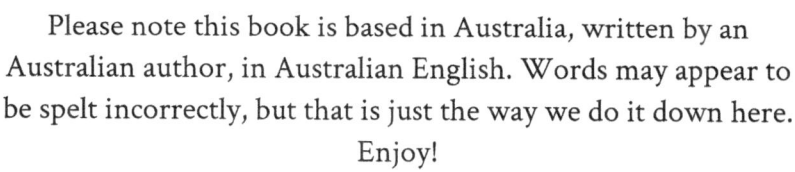

Please note this book is based in Australia, written by an Australian author, in Australian English. Words may appear to be spelt incorrectly, but that is just the way we do it down here. Enjoy!

PROLOGUE

Oliver

Eight years ago...

I AM ALMOST HOME FROM school when I see her. A small form, sitting on our front porch, head down, knees up with her arms wrapped around them. It's Lilly, my younger sister Amy's best friend and my friend too. We are two years apart in age. I'm eighteen, and Lilly is about to turn sixteen. She has been a part of our lives for as long as I can remember. Lilly and Amy have always been inseparable, and because of this, she is like a part of our family. Not that I think of her as a sister, but she has always been special to me. I approach her with caution, not wanting to spook her, as my mind races with questions. Why is she just sitting there, so still? Lilly is usually bouncing around, filled with energy. Is there something wrong with her? I approach her slowly and say in a soft voice, "Hey, Lil?"

Lilly looks up at me with tears swimming in her big blue eyes. And it hits me in the gut like a sucker punch. My heart stops and then races again; something is wrong! I crouch in front of her, asking with a sense of urgency, "Lilly? Are you OK? Are you hurt?"

She gives me a sad half smile and shakes her head. "I'm not hurt, Ol. Do you know where Amy is?"

As she's speaking, I frantically scan her from head to toe, still looking for injuries, and tell her, "Amy is at debate practice this afternoon. She should be home soon."

At this news, more tears fill her eyes, and seeing it has my stomach twisting and my hands clenching into fists. I'm going to find whoever hurt Lilly, and I'm going to hurt them back. Feeling protective of her, I sit next to her and, after some hesitation, put my arm around her shoulders. "I'm here now. Want to tell me what's wrong?"

Lilly lets out a soft sigh and snuggles in closer to me. I close my eyes for a brief moment and take in a deep breath, the scent of Lilly filling my lungs. Coconut and vanilla. She always smells sweet. Maybe it's all the baking she does?

"Zack Petty broke up with me today," she tells me in a small voice. Zack Petty, the little punk. That's who I need to find and hurt. How dare he make Lilly cry? And when did she start dating? And why does the thought of this make me feel so unsettled? Lilly is just my friend. Why am I feeling jealous all of a sudden? I get up to pace back and forth, my thoughts making me feel restless. "You've been dating Zack?"

Lilly lifts her head to watch me pace, her beautiful face soaked with tears. When did I start thinking of Lilly as beautiful?

"We've been together for a few weeks," she tells me in a shy voice, seeming embarrassed by this information. "And today he dumped me because he wants to ask Bianca Cooke out instead." At this, she cries again, and I stop pacing to pull her in for another hug. I try to ignore how good she feels in my arms and instead focus on making her feel better.

I squeeze her tight and tell her with complete sincerity, "Zack is a jerk. He does not deserve another tear from you."

Lilly looks up at me and hiccups into a smile. "You have to say that, Ol. You're my friend, and you must be on my side." The word friend coming out of Lilly's mouth feels wrong all of a sudden, but I force myself to move past it to focus on what she is saying.

"Lilly, listen to me. Zack is clearly a terrible guy, with awful judgment if he's choosing to be with someone like Bianca Cooke over you."

She looks back at me, letting out a disbelieving laugh. "Bianca Cooke is amazing. Her hair is straight, and her skin is flawless. She's smart and popular and is the captain of the dance team. Bianca is everything I'm not."

I stare at this amazing girl in front of me, taking in her wild, wavy brown hair, her deep-blue eyes, her newly curvy body—which I shouldn't be noticing so much—and I can't believe what she is saying. She does not see that she is more incredible, more beautiful, than Bianca Cooke could ever be.

I lift my hand and, with gentle fingers, wipe the tears from her cheek, noticing for the first time how soft her skin is, my fingers tingling as I touch her. This is all kinds of confusing. I clear my throat and lean away from her to gather my thoughts, and we sit together in silence for a bit.

"Ollie, tell me the truth. What's so wrong with me that he would reject me like this?" Lilly asks, breaking the silence and looking at me with her big, sad eyes, and I have to resist the urge to pull her close to me again.

"There is not one thing wrong with you, Lilly Hamilton. You are perfect." As soon as the words leave my mouth, I know with complete clarity that Lilly is perfect, the perfect girl for me. And as she smiles at me, a smile that is like the sun coming out from behind the clouds, I'm hit with the knowledge that I'm in love with my little sister's best friend. And oh boy, I am totally screwed.

CHAPTER 1

Lilly

Present day...

"COME ON, FRANKIE. NOT TODAY. Your time isn't up yet, bestie," I plead with my almost twenty-year-old Honda hatchback. "I just need you to give it one last push. We're almost home." I sigh as Frankie splutters, lets out her last pained breath, and goes quiet. So this is it. I'm officially stranded on the side of the road, in the dark no less, with 0 percent battery life on my phone, questioning again why these things always happen to me. Just last week, I locked myself out of this car (yes, Frankie is one of those old-fashioned gals who still needs a key to get into), and now this. Maybe the union for Honda cars got together and decided to go on strike against just me. Because there's no other way to explain the fact that this car and I aren't getting along so well these days. Only two weeks into the new year, and things are going downhill for me. Fast.

I attempt to pull myself together, leaving the internal lectures and plans to make up with the automotive industry for another day, and focus instead on how I'm going to get home. I take some small comfort in the fact that I at least managed to get Frankie safely off the road before she gave up her will to live. Given that I know less than nothing about the internal workings of car engines, I dismiss any thoughts of popping the hood and banging about in there. That would just be an exercise in futility. With no other immediate answers coming to mind, and no one in the vicinity to help me, I rest my head on the steering wheel and jump a mile when the horn blares.

"Well, it's good to know the horn still works," I mutter to myself while contemplating whether I can create enough noise with my horn to attract some attention. As I'm pondering if I should attempt Morse code for SOS using my car horn, a tap on my window has me jumping again.

"Are you OK in there? Do you need some help?"

I groan as I recognise that deep, masculine voice. Of course it would be him. What are the chances of him driving down this particular road at this particular time? The gods aren't playing nicely today.

"Oliver," I say in a casual voice, rolling down my window. "Can I help you?"

"Lilly?" Oliver, my best friend's older brother, frowns back at me. "Is that you? Are you OK?"

"Oh, sure, everything's fine. All under control here," I tell him in a cheerful voice.

With a perplexed look on his face, he asks, "What are you doing out here in the dark?"

A small, worried frown forms between his brows, and I hasten to reassure him that all is OK.

"Ummm, well, Frankie here appears to be having a teeny, tiny problem. I'm giving her some time and gentle encouragement, and I'm sure she'll rally at any moment now."

"Frankie? You named your car after a waitress in a fifties American diner?" he asks with a small smile, his sometimes serious demeanour softening.

"Hey, don't insult Frankie or she'll never wake up from her little nap," I tell him, patting the dashboard of my car in a soothing motion. "I'll be fine. No need for any help."

Oliver sighs, knowing full well that chances are he will need to help me.

"Come on, Lilly, hop out. I'll drive you home. I think we can both see that Frankie here is out for the night."

As Oliver steps back and opens my door, I get a good look at him. Why does he always have to look so well put together? Oliver is one of those people who has always had his life in order. From the time he graduated high school, he had a plan, and he stuck to it. University, degree, career. Next step will be marriage, some kids, and a white picket fence. I wince when I think of this. I can't picture Oliver married to someone. Else.

I shake myself out of these thoughts and notice, not for the first time, how damn good looking he is. Oliver was one of those lucky teenagers who never went through an awkward stage. He went from a skinny kid one day to a dreamboat the next. As we grew up together, I tried not to think of him in that way, tried fiercely to see him as an older brother type. But it never worked. Oliver with his deep-brown eyes, his strong jawline, and his wavy brown hair that does not seem to respond to humidity the way it's supposed to, has always been a fine-looking man in my eyes. Add in the fitted jeans and the polo shirt that hugs his shoulders just so, and well, here I am trying not to drool.

I glance down at my outfit, knowing that I don't look quite as well put together. My cut-off jean shorts and hot-pink (shrunk-in-the-wash) Hello Kitty T-shirt have seen better days. I'm sure what little make-up I applied this morning has melted off my face, and my hair? Well, it's best not to check what sort of mess the day has left that in.

"Lilly? Are you getting out?" Oliver asks with a hint of amusement mixed with annoyance in his voice as I sit here staring at him, mouth hanging open.

"Oh, sorry! Yes, coming." I curse Frankie under my breath as I gather my bag and step out of the car. As I look back at my now useless ex-best-friend Frankie, I glance at where Oliver is walking and curse again. Of course Emma is sitting in the front seat of Oliver's latest-model Lexus, looking on with frustration etched on her face. Oliver's girlfriend of almost ten months has never made a secret of the fact that both me and Amy, Oliver's little sister and my best friend, are constant sources of irritation in her life. I often wonder how the two of them are still together when Emma is so rude to the people in his life, but having observed them from afar over the course of their relationship, I've noticed she seems to only bring this side out on rare occasion. And when looking at Emma through an objective lens, I can admit she is pretty perfect. She has it all. And she manages to have it all together as well. And she suits Oliver. They are both high achievers with ambitions and goals. Go getters. Whereas I can't even get my car to go, let alone any other important parts of my life.

I smile to myself at my little pun and give Emma an apologetic wave as I trudge towards Oliver's car. As I approach, I notice Oliver is giving me a sweeping glance from head to toe and see him smile as he takes in my Hello Kitty T-shirt.

"What?" I ask him with as much dignity as I can muster as I step past him and into his car, bumping my head as I do so.

Oliver laughs as he runs his hand over my head in one soft motion and whispers back, "Nothing, kitty cat," in a teasing voice, low enough for only my ears. I laugh and try to ignore the goose-bumps that are always an inevitable response to any attention I receive from Oliver. I can't help it if my body enjoys the way he looks and sounds just a little bit too much.

"Sorry, Emma, for interrupting your night," I say as I settle myself into Oliver's immaculate car, rubbing my head, messing my hair up further.

"It's not a problem," Emma replies with an insincere smile, running her hand in a deliberate motion over her neat, pin-straight blonde hair. Subtle. "Oliver would have stopped for any-one stranded on the side of the road."

Huh, well, that put me in my place as no one special, which was Emma's intention, I know. As I glance up, I see Oliver grin-ning at me in the rear-view mirror.

"Only Lilly and Frankie would choose to have a falling out and break up at this inconvenient time," he jokes, and in my mind, I give him a little clap for this display of humour.

I flushed with embarrassment at Emma's jibe but am feeling somewhat placated by Oliver's attempt at a joke. I know he's trying to smooth over some of the sting from Emma's remarks, some-thing he has to do often, a fact that causes endless strife with Amy and Emma, both questioning where his loyalty lies. I don't get in-volved with this, though, always knowing where I stand with Oliver as annoying little sister 2.0. Silly Lilly, always a minute away from disaster. This is one of the reasons I have been keeping my distance from Oliver in recent months; I don't want to be a source of any conflict or discomfort in his life.

"So I'll take you home and you can organise a tow truck for Frankie?" Oliver asks, back to being pragmatic and serious while I revel inside at his continued use of my car's nickname.

"Sure, sounds good," I say, distracted now, my mind focused on what sugary treats I plan to bake when I get home. Should I make brownies or cookies or both? I've had a rough night. Both it is.

"Lilly," Oliver says in his stern, pay-attention voice. "You have to get this sorted tonight, OK?"

I nod and salute Oliver from behind his seat with a smile. "It will all get sorted, Ollie. No worries."

"You should have roadside assistance for these situations, Lacey," Emma pipes up, her voice dripping with condescension.

"It's Lilly," both Oliver and I correct her at the same time.

"And roadside assistance wouldn't have been an option today." I wave my lifeless phone in the air. "No way to call for help on this thing."

Oliver lets out a groan. Uh-oh, the ever-organised Oliver will not be happy with this information.

"Lilly, you need to be more diligent about these things. I may not always be around to rescue you."

"I should hope you won't," Emma agrees with a huff. Mean.

I sink lower in my seat as sadness fills me at the thought of Oliver not being around, popping up to get me out of a jam. Maybe I should plan for a life without disasters instead of lamenting losing the person to rescue me from said disasters? Hmm, interesting idea. Time for some New Year's resolutions, perhaps?

"Lilly, we're here." Oliver's voice pulls me out of my life-altering deliberations as I notice we've arrived at my apartment building. I look at Oliver's face and can see he's not happy with the neighbourhood I'm living in, in the outer suburbs of Melbourne, but hey, it's mine, and it's cheap!

"I'll walk you up," Oliver says in a determined voice, much to Emma's dismay.

"Really, Oliver? I'm sure Laney here is perfectly capable of making her way to her own apartment."

"Yes, Ollie," I parrot back to him. "Laney here is perfectly capable of walking to her own apartment. I think."

Oliver ignores both of us, giving me a look that says he doesn't believe I can walk the five hundred metres without incident—fair—and opens my car door, ushering me towards my building.

"Lilly, are you sure it's safe to live here?" he asks, looking around, his eyes wide with worry. I see the buildings and its surroundings through Oliver's eyes, and I guess it looks a little dodgy. There are a few rough-looking men gathered around in groups, staring at us as we walk by, and there always seems to be a car alarm or a police siren blaring in the distance. It's only a few suburbs over from where Oliver and Amy peacefully live, but in Melbourne, those few suburbs are the difference between houses with backyard swimming pools and apartments in high-crime areas. Unfortunately for me, I'm not in the former category.

"It's fine here, Ol," I attempt to reassure him. "I've made friends with Johnny over there." I point to the biggest man in the group. I guess when looking at Johnny without knowing him, he looks a bit scary, with his blue mohawk and tattoos, but the Johnny I know is a big teddy bear.

"Hi, Johnny!" I yell at him with a cheerful wave.

Johnny's angry-looking face breaks out into a big smile when he sees me.

"Hey, Lilly. Nice night, isn't it?" he says in his deep voice.

"Wonderful night," I say. "I'm going to bring you down some cookies that I'm planning to bake later tonight. Any requests?"

Johnny looks at me with pure joy at this. "Anything you make, Miss Lilly, I'm sure I'll love."

I nod and wave goodbye, grabbing Oliver, who's been watching this exchange with a look of bemused dismay.

"C'mon, Ollie. Let's get me safely to my front door," I say to him, a bit tongue in cheek, having just illustrated that I have my security in this building completely under control.

Oliver shakes his head and follows me, his hand on my lower back as he half guides me, half shields me to my front door.

"You see, I bring Johnny lots of my treats, and he looks out for me. It's been a good working relationship so far," I tell him, puffing out my chest a bit with pride.

Oliver has the decency to look somewhat impressed but is still looking around with nerves written on his face. Expecting what? I'm not sure.

"Make sure you lock your door after I leave," he tells me as I let myself into my apartment. "And don't forget to put the chain on."

"Yes, Dad," I say in a mocking tone, knowing his concern is coming from a good place but also resenting being treated like a kid.

"Thanks again for the rescue, Ollie," I add. "I don't know what I'd do without you."

"You won't ever need to find out. I'll always be here if you need me."

"Not if Ella out there has any say in the matter," I can't stop myself from saying. "The way she behaves, I think she would be OK if I ran into a bit of trouble with one of Johnny's friends out there."

"Never say that," Oliver admonishes me in a soft voice. "You will always be important to me." He looks at me for a long moment and then leans in for a hug. Ahh, a hug from Oliver is as close to bliss as possible, without including chocolate. He holds on for just a little longer than is necessary, and I revel in it every time.

"Goodnight, Lil," he says to me as he pulls away. "Lock up tight. And don't forget to call that tow truck," he adds, just to be annoying, as he is walking away.

"Bye, Ollie. Enjoy the rest of your night with Emilia," I sing-song back to him with a laugh.

Oliver stops and looks at me, flashes me his smile, the one with all the dimples, then turns to run down the stairs. And leaves me to sigh with a touch of longing as I turn and close the door. And lock it with the chain because I'm not a complete imbecile.

CHAPTER 2

Lilly

A FTER OLIVER LEAVES, I WALK further into my apartment, dropping my bag on the floor and flopping down onto my couch. I pick up a pen and notepad from my coffee table and write "call a tow truck" on my to-do list. I know I could just call them right now, on the spot, but as with any mundane task, I put it off in favour of doing something more fun. Like lying on the couch and pondering all my life choices. With my head resting on one of my soft throw cushions, I think about Oliver and our convoluted history of my running into trouble and Oliver running in to save me. It's been a permanent fixture in my life, ever since he was catapulted into mine, courtesy of Amy. On the first day of kindergarten, Amy sat down next to me, stole half my sandwich, and declared we'd be best friends forever. And she was right. We've been inseparable ever since. Every memory I have of growing up includes Amy by my side, and in the early days, Oliver was also there watching from the sidelines, helping us get out of any and every mess we made. As we got a bit older, we seemed to grow naturally apart, but that never stopped him from being there when I needed him.

As I think back, the first memory I have of Oliver as my knight in shining armour is when I was seven years old and the stinky Cameron Frankel had made me cry by calling me Silly Lilly in front of the entire class. Oliver, who was older and wiser than me, took the time to comfort me in the playground, sharing his cookies and telling me terrible jokes until I felt better. He was there for me when I was thirteen and my hamster, Buttons, the cutest hamster ever to live, had died an unexpected death. With my teenage hormones all over the place, I was so upset that I couldn't bring myself to study for my upcoming maths exam. With the idea of a failing grade almost inevitable, Oliver, the maths nerd, stepped in, sitting up with me for half the night to make sure I was ready for the test the next day. I got a C+ for our efforts, so it had all been worth it. And when at the tender age of sixteen, I experienced my first heartbreak at the hands of Zack Petty, who dumped me for the more popular, better-looking Bianca Cooke, who had bigger boobs than me, it was Oliver's shoulder I cried on. I can't remember a time when I needed him and he wasn't there. Even when he went away to study at university, he stayed in my life. I recall the one time when he dropped everything to come and get me when my ex-boyfriend Sebastian broke up with me while we were on a romantic weekend away, leaving me stranded in a cabin on a snow-capped mountain. Oliver was the one who got in his car and drove the three hours to pick me up after Amy couldn't find a way to get to me. And he let me listen to sad Ed Sheeran songs all the way home while feeding me chocolates. And in doing all this, over all these years, he has been owning, bit by bit, pieces of my heart. Unfortunately for me, given how well structured Oliver's life is, with a strict ten-year plan in place, in contrast to the chaotic nature of my life, I cannot imagine I own any part of his.

OK, time to snap out of this trip down Oliver's memory lane and focus on more positive things, like baking. For as long as I can remember, baking has been a cathartic experience for me. When I'm in the kitchen, assembling ingredients and creating new treats, any stress or angst I'm feeling melts away like butter. I can always rely on losing myself in flour and sugar and chocolate. There's not a single world problem that I believe cannot be solved with chocolate.

When I was fourteen years old, I fell in love with baking. I had enrolled in a home economics class at school to get out of taking any other, "serious" electives, and it was love at first bite. I fell in love with my whole heart. It was one of the few classes at school that I looked forward to each week, and I would spend hours at home in the evenings or on the weekends trying out new recipes to get better at it. My parents, being more academically inclined, saw this as nothing more than a fun hobby of mine, not understanding how much being in the kitchen, creating new flavour profiles, soothed my soul. In the kitchen, I felt in control, as opposed to in every other facet of my life. I had thought my dad would appreciate this, given how similar cooking is to his line of work. Until earlier this year, my dad spent most of his career working in a research laboratory, following scientific protocols, similar to what I do when I follow a recipe. To me, making the perfect crème brûlée is a form of science, where every ingredient is exact and every step precise. When I told this to my parents, they laughed, not in a mean way but in a dismissive one, so I decided way back then to keep my passion for food as only a hobby and tried to find a more serious path in life. Upon reflection, this hasn't gotten me anywhere good.

When this feeling of melancholy threatens to overpower me, I decide to do something more productive with my thinking time.

After that embarrassing car ride home with the judgy Emma and the so well-put-together Oliver, I'm suddenly sick of being the only adult in our group to not be fully grown up yet. I keep circling from one disaster to the next, and perhaps it's time to do something about it. I know I'm capable of being more than what I am now, the person who floats through life, making messes and hoping someone will be around to help clean them up.

With this determination to be better in mind, I'm filled with a sudden surge of energy to do something proactive about it. I am twenty-three years old, after all. Maybe it's time to rein in the chaos and take charge of my life. I spy the to-do list on my coffee table, pick it up, and add to it in earnest. First comes a title: New Year's Resolutions—How to Get Lilly's Life in Order. Then item number one: Get a new job. This to me is a no brainer. At the moment, I work as a secretary (aka general dogsbody) at a testosterone-filled real estate office. I wandered into this job soon after leaving university, having graduated with a bachelor's degree in business studies (of all things), and with a complete lack of a career plan. To pay for things like rent and food and bills, I accepted an offer from the first place willing to hire me and have been stuck there ever since. And the place is awful. The men working there seem to think I'm their mother (no, I won't take your clothes to the laundromat) or their personal pin-up doll (no, I don't want to pose as a "model" for your "photographer" friend). The place does not foster a healthy working environment.

When I picture what my ideal career looks like, it has always involved baking. And wouldn't it be great if I can find a job that merges my passion for food with a way to make money? Maybe I can open and run a little bakery/café filled with all my favourite treats, and it would be a place where friends can meet and hang out in a comfortable, welcoming environment. Like Rachel and

Chandler and Joey and the gang at Central Perk. The more I think about this, the more I warm to the idea. I could call it the Love, Lilly café. Where every treat is made with love. Wow, only a few minutes of thinking and I know I'm onto a winner with this idea.

OK, so number two on my to-do list is to figure out how to make this dream job a reality. No big deal, two super simple things to start with. Now number three: Find a better place to live. Despite my assurances to Oliver, this place isn't safe, my working relationship with Johnny notwithstanding. I often think it's lucky that Frankie is so old and prone to frequent unplanned naps; otherwise, she may not have lasted too long parked in this neighbourhood. The trouble with this item on the to-do list is the money I make at my crappy job only allows me to live in a place like this, where the rent is low because it's subsidised by a small amount of perpetual fear. Hmmm, tricky.

And last but not least, number four on my list, move on from this teeny, tiny, little Oliver crush and find a boyfriend who is in my league. Oliver has been an unattainable fantasy crush for my entire adult life, and it's time to grow up and be realistic about my love life. I need to find someone who is more suited to my brand of doing life. And despite this current attempt at being normal, let's face it, there's a chance I'll stumble on to-do list item number one, so it's best to find someone who embraces the chaos.

Now that I have my thoughts out in the open, with a plan in place, I feel a bit better about the future. I get excited at the thought of ticking things off my list and am pleased just to have made a road map for myself to get out of the rut I've been living in. With that now sorted for the moment, I can head to the kitchen to work on the cookies I'm planning to make for Oliver. A thank-you and a "sorry for ruining your evening" batch of Love, Lilly cookies. And maybe I'll make some for Amy as well, while I'm here. And don't forget the "for safe keeping" cookies for Johnny. I have a busy night ahead. With a big smile, I take out the required flour and sugar and butter. I put on some soft music in the background and get lost in the pleasure of creating something from scratch with love.

When I wake the next morning, with a slight sugar hangover—I may or may not have overindulged in a little bit of raw cookie dough—I attempt to make myself presentable. I start by working on my hair, always the trickiest part of getting ready. My hair is medium length, wavy—OK, frizzy—and loves to expand in volume with any hint of humidity. After I end up tying it in a high ponytail, I put on a pair of shorts, a black tank top, and a bit of mascara and lip gloss to jazz up my face, then get ready to leave. Almost out of the door, I stop short, having glanced at my list, and backtrack to my computer to find a local tow truck to rescue Frankie. I hope she can forgive me for leaving her out there alone all night. Now that I have that all sorted, I gather up my baked goods and head out again. Only to reach the bottom of the stairs and realise I have no means of transportation. Sometimes I take a while to join the dots—tow truck to get Frankie means no car, Lilly!

I wave to Johnny, who it would seem hasn't left his spot loitering in front of the building, and deposit a box filled with double chocolate chip cookies into his hands. They're his favourite. Johnny opens the box with glee and takes a big sniff.

"Lilly, these smell like heaven." He picks me up and crushes me in a big hug.

I thank Johnny and get back to the problem at hand. No transportation. As I glance around, I spot my old bike resting against the side of the building. About six months ago, I bought this bike during a fitness fad and used it a grand total of one time. Who knew cycling long distances was so hard? Since then, the bike has remained rusting in the sun, the rundown state of it the only reason it hasn't been stolen yet. I look at the tyres with doubt, giving them a feeble kick, and try to think of another option. An Uber is too expensive, especially given how much the tow truck company is charging me to get Frankie, and I can't ask Oliver to come and pick me up to get his thank-you gift, because that seems redundant, so riding the bike it is.

"What do you think, Johnny? Is this thing going to get me where I need to go?"

Johnny frowns at my sad-looking bike and says with a cautious nod, "Just don't go too fast, Miss Lil. And try to stay on the footpath. Avoid cars!"

I take this advice to heart, and after putting my two Tupperware containers in the pink basket at the front of the bike, I hop on and wobble for a bit. With a wave to Johnny, who is still watching me with a worried frown, I say a little prayer to the gods from yesterday who forsook me and now owe me one and start peddling. It's not that far to Amy and Oliver's house. How hard can this be?

CHAPTER 3

Lilly

ONE HOUR AND A BUCKET of sweat later, I arrive puffed and dishevelled at the Harlow house. It's hot today, which is pretty standard for this time of year. I don't know why I thought cycling anywhere in the middle of summer was a good idea, but here we are. What started out as a fresh outfit is now drenched in sweat, and my hair is at least twice its normal size. Not that I should care too much about what I look like. This family has seen me in much worse conditions. A case in point is the time I had a mutant bout of the chicken pox and looked like a creature dredged up from the deepest blue sea. That was a rough week! And then there was that weekend of food poisoning a few years back, after I dismissed the concerns of those around me and binged on gas station sushi at 1:00 a.m. Let's just say Amy and Oliver did not see me looking my best that night. So I guess being a little bit sweaty—OK, maybe a lot sweaty—isn't so bad in the grand scheme of things. I just wouldn't mind, this one time, looking at least presentable in Oliver's presence.

Before I enter, giving my sweat some time to dry on my skin (gross), I stop to admire the split-level house in front of me. It's a gorgeous cottage-style home, with a white weatherboard facade and cute planter boxes in front of the windows. It also has an old-fashioned wraparound porch in the front, complete with a delightful timber swing. The Harlow family has lived here forever, and when six months ago, Amy and Oliver's parents re-tired and moved to a small town a few hours away, closer to the mountains and with a more temperate climate, they let their adult children remain in the family home, living rent free in the lap of luxury. Lucky kids! They don't have to deal with the likes of Johnny to feel safe in their home, not that I mind Johnny that much, and maybe even consider him a friend of sorts. Anyway, once I'm feeling drier, hoping my deodorant holds up today, I de-cide it may be safe to enter. I balance the cookies in one hand, knocking on the door of the house that is like a second home to me, and hope against hope that it's Amy and not Oliver who will open the door.

"Lilly? Are you OK?" Of course it's Oliver again. The gods must be angry with me at the moment. I need to remember to do something charitable in the next few days to get them back on my side. Also, Oliver is looking at me with a high level of alarm, so I can just imagine how bad I must look.

"Hi, Ollie! I come bearing gifts." I point to the Love, Lilly cookies in my hands.

"Come from where?" he asks. "The sun?"

Standing back, he moves to allow me to enter, and as always, he gives me a sweeping glance from head to toe, like he's checking for injuries or something.

Uncomfortable with his gaze on me, I shift from side to side, wishing I could do something to magically fix my appearance.

"Funny guy! I had to ride my bike, as Frankie isn't in working condition, remember? And before you ask," I continue, interrupting his obvious next question, "I've organised a tow truck, and they're picking her up as we speak."

"You rode all the way here in this heat?" he asks, concern replacing his amusement. "You should have called me. I would have come and got you."

"And then I would have had to bake you some more cookies, and the cycle continues."

"Right, well, come in. The air conditioning is on, and I'll grab you some water."

I follow Oliver into the kitchen. "Thanks, Ollie. And here, I baked you your favourite cookies—double chocolate chip with extra M&M'S." I smile as he grabs the cookies from me before shoving two into his mouth as he fills up a glass of water for me.

"Thanks, Lil. But you know you don't have to give me anything. Helping you is like a hobby of mine." It does seem to keep him busy, I think to myself.

"Well then, let me take them back." I go to grab the cookies off him.

"Don't you dare," he says as he cradles the cookies protectively to his chest. "They're mine!"

As I sit down at the kitchen counter with my glass of water in hand, I take the time to admire, as I always do, the size of the kitchen in front of me. With the granite benchtops and the industrial-size stove top and oven, I can only dream about the number of quality baked foods I could create in this space. All the spotless stainless-steel appliances are screaming out for me to make a mess in my eternal quest for the perfect brownie.

"So what other disasters have you got planned for today?" Oliver jokes, sitting down next to me, breaking me out of my silent coveting of his kitchen.

"There's a house fire I'm planning to light a little later, but that's not until after lunch, so I have some time," I quip back, earning the full-dimple smile from Oliver.

"Is Amy here? I have some cookies for her as well," I ask, tearing my eyes from his deadly dimples.

"She should be back from her night shift any minute now," he says, looking at the clock on the wall. "Feel free to hang out until she gets back." Amy works as a nurse in the emergency department at Mercy Hospital, a major metropolitan hospital in the city, and often works crazy hours.

I spy Oliver's laptop open on the bench, noting that he must be working on a Saturday. "I can wait in her room, if you have plans?" I don't want to be in the way.

Oliver also glances at his laptop, and after a moment's hesitation, he says, "No, no plans. Just doing some work to get ahead for the week I have coming up. No big deal. You can stay right here and catch me up on your life. It's been ages since I've gotten to have a real chat with you."

"You've been busy," I tell him in a droll voice. "You know, with Emily?"

"Ha ha," he laughs. "We don't spend that much time together."

I give him a sceptical look, knowing from Amy that Oliver splits his time almost solely between work and Emma.

"Well, I've been busy too. I've made a few New Year's resolutions that I'm working on."

With a pointed look at the calendar, clearly showing that it is already the sixteenth of January, Oliver says, "A little late getting started on those this year?"

"Maybe I should add that to my resolutions? Get a calendar? And be less tardy?" I say with a cheeky smile.

Oliver laughs at this, so I continue.

"My primary focus is to put into motion some plans to open a café or bakery one day. Soon. Because I simply can't continue to work for those Neanderthals at O'Brien/O'Ryan Real Estate."

Oliver gets that protective look in his eyes and asks not for the first time since I started working at O'Brien/O'Ryan Real Estate, "Are those guys still bothering you?"

I smile at this and downplay just how bad that place is in reality. "It's not always bad. It's just that given I'm only one of two women working there, they rarely know what to do with me, always giving me the most ridiculous tasks to complete, and the younger ones are always asking me out to drinks, no matter how many times I tell them I'm not interested."

At this, Oliver's jaw clenches, and he tells me in a serious voice, "Lilly, they can't do that. It's harassment. Talk to your manager. Get him to sort it out."

I look away as he says that, all of a sudden very interested in a painting on the wall.

"Lilly, is your manager one of these men not taking no for an answer?" he asks, his face turning a little pink, maybe with frustration.

"It doesn't matter," I reassure him, "because I have a plan to get out."

"A plan?" Oliver asks, still looking somewhat cross.

"Yes, I'm putting together a plan to open my café," I announce.

"And by putting together a plan...?" he asks me in an all-knowing tone.

"OK, so currently I'm just putting out some good vibes," I tell him, laughing, knowing that making and sticking to plans isn't a strength of mine.

"You know I love your cookies and treats, Lilly. You're an exceptional baker," he tells me. "Have you ever thought about doing a pop-up café stall at the local shopping centre? As a starting point? Clients of mine from the firm rave about the success they've had by keeping things small to begin with."

"A pop-up café?" I echo, feeling butterflies dance with excitement in my stomach. "That sounds perfect!" I grin at Oliver, filled with gratitude that he's not only taking my dreams seriously but also finding a way for me to make them happen. Oliver is a proper grown up with an actual career, so to have him buy into my plans for a café fills me with purpose and self-satisfaction. Things I haven't felt in a long time.

"Do you think I can make it work?" I ask.

"You can do anything you put your mind to, Lil," he says with confidence. "And besides, these cookies will sell themselves," he adds as he munches on his third one of the day.

"This is so great. Now I have something tangible to focus on. Thank you, Ollie," I say as I launch myself at him for a grateful hug. Oliver grabs me, squeezes me, and holds me close for one, two, three...ten seconds this time. Wow, these Oliver hugs are getting longer. For a man who isn't prone to acts of overt affection, he sure knows how to give a wonderful hug.

"You're welcome," he says as I plunk myself back onto my stool. Is Oliver closer than he was before? "I didn't really do anything. But I'm happy to help with anything you may need. Some marketing tips, perhaps?" Oliver has just been promoted to senior brand manager at his fancy marketing company, so he could be of use here.

"I can't afford you, Ollie," I remind him with a smile.

"Just keep me filled with sugary treats and you will have me forever," he replies.

I feel my smile wobble as I digest his words. If only I could have him forever. As I look at his lips with longing, Oliver leans forward. I hold my breath as his fingers reach towards my face. What is happening?

"You have a bit of something smudged right here." He wipes gently at what must be the mascara smeared under my eye. Great, here I was thinking we were having a moment, and he's trying to stop me looking like a racoon. Good going, Lilly.

I lean away from him and, using my forefingers, rub under my eyes.

"Thanks! Sorry you've had to look at me sitting here like a hot mess all this time." My face is flaming with embarrassment. I wish I were a different sort of person sometimes, someone who can get through the day without parts of her make-up melting down her face.

At this, Oliver's eyebrows pinch together in consternation as he looks at my face, his eyes skating over my lips and flushed cheeks. Great, what else do I have running down my face?

"Lilly...," he starts.

"Lilly? Are you here?" comes the booming voice of my best friend, Amy, bouncing into the house. "Is that a bike I see outside?" she asks, sounding perplexed. She skids to a halt as she enters the kitchen, her big brown eyes narrowing in suspicion as she perhaps notices the weird vibe between me and Oliver.

"What's going on here?" she asks, pulling her long brown hair into a messy ponytail, her eyes darting between the two of us.

I clear my throat and sit back on my stool, moving even further away from Oliver.

"Nothing! I just brought some treats to thank Oliver for rescuing me last night."

Amy opens her mouth to ask more questions, and I beat her to it.

"Don't ask," I say. "Just another one of my Silly Lilly incidents. I'll fill you in later."

"OK," she says, still looking at us with a hint of suspicion.

"Look, I bought you some treats too!" I hold up the second Tupperware container to distract her. It works.

"Are they mint chocolate chip cookies?" she asks with obvious delight.

"Would I dare to bring you anything else?"

"Not if you want to keep best friend status. Come on, let's go to my room. I need to get out of these scrubs. And you need to fill me in on some things, starting with that bike outside," she says. As she ushers me out of the room, I turn to see Oliver watching me leave, a small frown on his face.

"Bye, Ollie. Thanks for the chat," I say as I walk out the door.

"See you soon, Lilly," is his soft reply.

CHAPTER 4

Lilly

"So spill, Miss Lil," Amy says as we close the door to her bedroom. I move the pile of books that are taking up half her bed, clearing some space for me to sit down. Amy is a voracious reader, a real bookworm, and as such, she always has well-worn paperbacks scattered around her room.

"What's been going on? And what did I just interrupt down there?" she asks.

"Nothing exciting, Ames. Just another Lilly incident that Oliver had to rescue me from." I fill her in on all the details from the Frankie situation last night, telling her about the ride home with Emma and the bike ride here this morning.

"Ugh, that Emma is the worst!" Amy declares when I'm finished. "Why is she always so condescending? And rude? She seemed so nice when they got together, and now she's turning into a real cow!"

"Beats me," I say. "I don't really know her all that well. All I know is that she's with Oliver. She has nothing to be upset about."

I shut my mouth at this as I realise what I've said, and Amy gives me a knowing smile. She has always suspected that I have a tiny crush on her big brother, but being the good friend that she is, she's kind enough not to bring it up very often.

"She's jealous of you, Lil. That's why she's extra mean when you're around."

"Jealous? Of me? I'm a hot mess. That makes no sense."

Amy huffs in frustration as she stands up and grabs me, pointing me to her full-length mirror.

"Yes, Lilly. Jealous of you. Look at you. You are pretty without even trying. I know you hate your 'frizzy' hair," she says, putting air quotes around the word frizzy. "But it's the sort of beach hair that women spend tonnes of money to get. And you have the nicest blue eyes, so much better than my boring brown ones. And don't get me started on that little body of yours, small waist, big boobs, skinny without needing to exercise. If I didn't love you so much, I'd hate you for that alone." When I go to interrupt her little pep talk, she puts her hand up to stop me. "And in addition to all the physical stuff, you have the sweetest heart of any person I've ever met. You know that if you weren't so amazing, Madi, Sammi, and I wouldn't still be friends with you after all these years!"

Amy is referencing Madeline Russell and Samantha Brown, the other two members in our small but mighty friendship group. The four of us have grown up together, and though the pressures of adulting often keep us from seeing one another regularly, like we did when we were in university, we still talk and text almost every day. We're ride or die friends, there for each other through the good and the bad.

As I take in what Amy has just said about my appearance, I look at myself in the mirror, filled with self-doubt. My so-called beach hair is now in a lopsided ponytail, having not survived unscathed the bike ride from hell. And, even after Oliver's attempts to help, my eyes still look like those of a racoon!

With this reflection in my sight, knowing that Amy perhaps has exaggerated somewhat my "pretty without trying" appearance, I look back at Amy with gratitude. Only a best friend could believe something so untrue. She has her biased best-friend blinders on.

"Thanks, Amy. But if I looked like what you've just described, wouldn't I have men clamouring to be with me?" I gesticulate with my arms. "And yet here I am, almost twenty-four and chronically single. No clamouring in sight."

Amy looks at me with sympathy and replies, "I think the men are clamouring, but you're too blinded by something, or someone, to notice them."

I think about this for a moment and then shake my head in disagreement.

"I just think that maybe I'm not the type of girl that men want to settle down with. My life is such I mess, I have no actual career, and in general, I'm surrounded by chaos. Who would want that? From where I'm sitting, men seem to want women who are well put together, with their life in order." And as I glance in the mirror again, taking in my crazy hair, thinking of Emma's dead-straight, humidity-defying, shiny blonde hair, I add, "And with straight, tidy hair."

As Amy goes to answer this, no doubt with more compliments and encouragement over what is a hopeless situation, I change the subject. "So how's work going? How are things with Dr McHottie?"

Amy has a contentious relationship—some may call it an almost full-out war—with the doctor who works in the emergency department with her, the one she was hitting on the fateful night of my twenty-third birthday, and the tales of their bust-ups are legendary. He went from a potential hook up to 100 percent nemesis in no time at all.

Amy looks at me, knowing I'm attempting to distract her, and takes pity on me. "Not great," she says. "He's still always around. Micromanaging me like he's my boss. We established early on that the nurses don't report to the doctors, yet he finds reasons to be all up in my face all day long."

I smile, looking at my gorgeous friend with her long brown hair, high cheekbones, and almond-shaped, big brown eyes, so like Oliver's, and can take a guess why this doctor wants to be in her face all day long. And remembering his enamoured look at the bar that night, I think maybe the good doctor is happy to be close to Amy, even if it means constantly fighting.

"He wants to shake up the way we work down in the emergency room," she continues with exasperation.

"What's wrong with how you work in the emergency room?" I ask as I plunk myself down on Amy's bed and roll over to face her, giving her my undivided attention.

"Nothing! There's nothing wrong with the way we run the department. He's just another man who thinks he knows better." I note that Amy, my very relaxed, nice-to-everyone, sometimes crazy but never angry best friend, is getting pretty worked up over this guy, a guy she claims to hate, but decide against saying anything to her about it. Who am I to give advice on matters of the heart, anyway?

"Do you want me to go so you can sleep?" I ask instead, sitting up, knocking over the tower of books resting precariously on her bedside table. As we both work to pick them up, Amy's face lights up with inspiration.

"No! Let's go swimming instead. I know I need to catch up on some sleep, but it's too nice today to be stuck in a dark room.

Besides, we both need some sunshine to increase our melatonin levels and help synchronise our circadian rhythms." When Amy speaks like this, it's a stark reminder of what a little genius she is. She's like a walking, talking encyclopedia of random facts. It's the reason my parents love her so much; she is more suited to be their daughter than I am.

I shake off this unhappy and potentially unfair thought and look out of the window. The Harlow house has a gorgeous kidney-shaped pool in the backyard, where it's now sitting pretty with its blue water glistening in the sunlight, beckoning for me to come in.

"I don't have a swimsuit," I remind Amy.

"You can borrow one of mine." She gets up to rummage through her drawers.

"Umm, Ames, I hate to point this out to you again," I say as she holds up a hot pink bikini in front of her face, looking at me and then back at the bikini. "But my C cups will not fit in those wisps of triangles."

"Who cares?" she replies. "It's just us. I've seen you in less."

I shrug, knowing this is true and now also keen for a dip, the cool waters of the pool calling my name, and grab the bikini from her, entering her en suite to change.

"Don't take too long!" she yells after me. "I'm dying to go swimming!" This is so like Amy; once a thought enters her mind, it has to happen right now.

I squeeze into the pink bikini top, and with a dubious look down, I see my boobs spilling out over the top.

"I look indecent," I mutter to myself as I walk out of the bath-room.

"You look hot!" Amy says at almost the same time.

I take in my image again in Amy's full-length mirror, and I smile when I see that at least my bottom half is somewhat covered. I shrug, tucking a wayward nipple back into the bikini top, and turn to Amy.

"You get out there and sunscreen up while I get changed," she says with sudden urgency, grabbing me by the shoulders and pushing me out of her room before shutting the door behind me.

"What's the rush, Ames?" I ask, looking behind me at the closed door and at the same time taking a step forward.

"Ooof." Smack bang into a solid wall of chest muscles.

"Lilly? Are you OK?" Oliver asks for what feels like the tenth time that day, his hands spanning my waist as he stops me from falling. Then those same big hands just seem to stay in place. His thumb stroking softly up and down my stomach, burning my skin in its wake. Oliver pulls me closer for one, two, three…twelve seconds this time. I stand there pressed against Oliver for twelve glorious seconds, neither of us in a hurry to move.

"Did you just smell me?" Oliver asks, leaning back to look at me with a confused smile on his face. I was sniffing him. He just smells so good. Woodsy, with hints of vanilla. A potent mix.

"No!" is my quick reply, my cheeks burning because I was so busted. "I was just trying to get a breath in with you holding me so tightly," I throw back at him.

Immediately his hands drop away from me as he clears his throat. "Sorry, Lil," he says as he looks down at his hands like they betrayed him, clenching them into fists.

"It's OK," I reply, trying to lighten the mood. "You were just making sure I don't fall down the stairs…again." I grimace as I remember the Christmas incident four years ago, where after too many glasses of wine, I fell down the stairs, earning me four stitches on my right elbow and a few notches down in my dignity.

Oliver lets out a small laugh as he no doubt remembers the same thing.

"Yes, that's right. Rescuing you again." His eyes crinkle as he smiles at me, his dimple flashing and disappearing as he takes in my barely-there-bikini-clad form.

"Going swimming?" he asks dumbly, swallowing hard, trying and failing to stop his gaze from wandering up and down my body. Interesting. In normal circumstances, Oliver's powers of observation are better than this.

"Yep," I say, popping the p. "Amy thinks we need some more melatonin or some other mumbo-jumbo. I wasn't really listening."

Oliver grins at me and moves to the side, gesturing down the stairs. "Need any help to manoeuvre these today?" he asks.

"I shall be OK today, kind sir," I say with a slight curtsy, my boobs almost falling out of my top as I do so.

With Oliver seemingly unable to glance away from this said area, I step around him and sashay down the stairs. When I get to the bottom, I look back up to see Oliver still there, staring after me, running his hands through his hair, something he does when he's feeling stressed.

"Have a nice afternoon, Ol. Hope you get some work done," I throw over my shoulder in a casual voice.

"That doesn't seem likely now," is his muttered, grumpy response.

CHAPTER 5

Lilly

A s I lounge on my inflatable pool chair, I float weightlessly around the cool water of the pool. This is pure bliss. After the stress of my car breaking down and the treacherous bike ride here this morning, this is exactly what I need. With my eyes closed against the bright sunshine, I picture Oliver's face as he looked at my body just before this. Could it be that part of Oliver is attracted to me? Or was it just a male response, one that could happen to any guy holding any half-naked girl in his arms? I think about Oliver's girlfriend now and try to focus on the fact that he is unavailable and unattainable to me. Yes, he may notice me as a woman from time to time, but that doesn't change the fact that he's happily coupled up with a woman who is very much my polar opposite. Emma, besides being beautiful and smart, is polished and well put together. She's always dressed in the latest fashion, never seems to spill food on herself (how's that even possible?), has a grown-up job as a junior legal associate at some big law firm, and is everything I hope to be when I grow up. I, on the other hand, can often not make it through the day without ripping an item of clothing, I'm always late for everything (including making New Year's resolutions), and I have a job that could be performed by a well-trained monkey. How could Amy ever think that Emma would be jealous of me?

SPLASH!

I shriek as a tidal wave knocks me off my floating lounge chair and I'm dunked without ceremony under the water. When I resurface spluttering, Oliver is grinning at me, his face filled with mischief. Again, so different from the Oliver I often get to see these days.

"What are you doing?" I sputter. "Are you trying to drown me?" I demand, splashing him in the face with a handful of water.

He laughs as he lunges for me, grabbing me, holding my hands still, and tells me, "I just walked past Amy's room. She's out cold on her bed." He adds, "Dressed in her bikini."

I laugh at the mental image of Amy passed out in her swimsuit.

"Oh, OK," I say. "That doesn't explain why you're out here, trying to kill me while I'm innocently trying to relax."

"I didn't want you to be lonely," he replies, letting go of me to swim to the other side of the pool. "You looked so sad out here all by yourself."

"Still doesn't explain the dunking," I mutter. "But I guess you can stay and hang out with me," I add, delighted to get to spend more time with him. Three Oliver encounters in two days. How did I get so lucky?

"Gee, thanks for giving me permission to use my swimming pool."

"Oh, shut up!" I grab him as he swims by, trying to force him underwater.

"Seriously, Lilly? Are you trying to dunk me? You, who can't stand with your head above water in the shallow end," he taunts me, referencing my lack of height. "Want to take me on?"

"You're going down, Oliver Harlow!" I declare, never one to back down from a challenge. I wrap my arms and legs around him from behind, wearing him like I'm his backpack, and attempt to use my body weight to drag us both backwards and underwater. It's a suicide mission, one might say, but well worth it if I succeed.

Unfortunately, there's no moving Oliver, who has become a man mountain. The water is causing a slippery friction between our bodies as I twist and turn on his back, and yes, maybe I'm enjoying this game a little too much. However, it would seem that Oliver isn't as keen on playing and isn't budging at all. In fact, he's now almost unnaturally still.

"Ollie?" I stop my thrashing about. "Am I hurting you?"

I climb off his back and swim around to face him, where Oliver is looking anywhere but at me, his cheeks red.

"Hey, did you put on sunscreen?" I ask, distracted by his possible sudden sunburn. Strange given he has only been out here for five minutes.

"Hmm?" he answers, glancing at me and then away again as I tread water in front of him. "Yes, I put sunscreen on. Thanks for your concern."

His face has returned to its normal olive complexion, so I let it go, instead focusing on the man in front of me. When did Oliver turned into this god? I mean, he was always fit, but from the looks of him today, Oliver's muscles have developed muscles. How does he fit in the time to exercise during what I know must be a sixty-hour work week for him? I feel my cheeks heat as I pry my eyes away from his impressive six (eight?) pack and swim towards the shallow end of the pool, trying to gain some distance from him. Oliver seems to have other ideas, and he follows right behind me, like my shadow. Once on solid ground, now able to stand in waist-high water, I look at him again and squeak, "Been hitting the gym recently?" Nice way to play it cool, Lilly.

Oliver's grin warms my insides as he gives me a knowing look and flexes his biceps. "Like what you see?" he teases.

"Oh, sure, it's fine. If you're into that kind of thing."

"What? You don't like men with muscles?" he asks with interest.

"Ummm?" I pretend to think about it while giving myself the excuse to look him up and down. "I guess muscles are all right. Me personally, I prefer a dad bod on a man, one that won't make me feel bad about my lack of a gym body."

Oliver raises an eyebrow as he returns the favour, letting his gaze travel up and down my body, lingering on my chest and stomach. To my utter embarrassment, my nipples tighten under his gaze, and as I attempt to hide my reaction to him, Oliver's gaze zeroes in on them.

"Lilly, I don't think there is a single thing wrong with your body," he tells me in a gruff voice, his eyes now fixed with determination on the blue sky above us.

I stare at Oliver in shock, covering my rebellious nipples by crossing my arms over my chest, forcing my boobs upward. Did Oliver just admit that he likes my body? As I grapple with what this could mean, Oliver grabs my head and submerges us both underwater, which is good for me because I need to cool off.

When we emerge, some of the weird tension between us has dissipated, and Oliver suggests we have a swimming race. This is the Oliver that I remember growing up with, the boy who was serious but always open to having fun. That Oliver doesn't make an appearance all that often any more.

"Oliver," I whine, wanting to play with him while he's in this mood but also wanting to choose an activity that exerts the least amount of energy. After the torturous bike ride this morning, floating in the pool sounds preferable to a swimming race. "Why must you always be so intent on being active? Why can't we lie on the pool lounges and take a nap instead?"

"Lilly." He mimics my whining. "You can relax later. Now we must find out which one of us will keep or win the Summer Champion Trophy."

I roll my eyes in pretend annoyance and think back to the many summers when all the neighbourhood kids would gather in this pool and compete for this trophy. When I look back now, it was only ever me and Oliver who took it seriously, and for me it was never about winning but was a chance to be close to Oliver. Looks like some things never change.

"You are on!" I state. "Two laps, up and back, and I get a head start because I come with a handicap."

"What handicap?"

"I have about a foot less in body length than you do, remember?"

He smiles back at me, his eyes crinkling against the sun.

"OK, I'll let you start further down the pool. Does that suit you, Your Highness?

"That will be fine," I reply in my very best fancy Bridgerton accent. I'm obsessed with that show. We smile at each other and take our positions in the pool.

"On your mark, get set, GO!" Oliver cries as we launch ourselves forward. Despite my getting off to a good start, in a flash Oliver has caught up to me, and by the turn of the first lap, he has pulled ahead.

Bollocks! I think to myself, still in Bridgerton mode. Must catch him.

As Oliver whizzes by me, I put in one last effort, closing the gap until I'm almost alongside him, and OOF!

I go under as I become a victim of a kick straight to the chest.

"Son of a bitch," I gasp as I resurface, sucking in some air.

"Lilly!" Oliver calls out, looking frantic, grabbing me and wrapping my legs around his waist, holding all my weight.

"Ouch," I moan, resting my head on his chest in a pathetic gesture.

Oliver, still looking panicked, swims us both to the shallow end and places me with care on the edge of the pool before hoisting himself out. When he goes to pick me up and carry me to the adjacent sun lounges, I snap out of my daze.

"Ollie. I'm fine," I wheeze.

He doesn't seem to hear me, his face pinched with worry, as he lifts me into his arms and deposits me into a chair.

"Lilly, do you need a doctor? Should I go in and wake up Amy? Are you OK?" Oliver looks at me, a worried expression marring his handsome face.

"I'm OK," I gasp, trying with a small amount of desperation to find the wind that was knocked out of my lungs. "It's fine, Ollie, give me a minute to catch my breath." When I look up, Oliver is staring at my chest again, and as I follow his gaze, I see a big, angry red mark where he kicked me.

"It was an accident, Ol," I say when he continues to stare at it. "I'll be fine."

Oliver shakes his head as he gets up to pace back and forth.

"Are you sure we shouldn't wake Amy? What if I've fractured one of your ribs? Or worse?" He looks so concerned that I grab his hand.

"It's just a bruise. I'm OK. See? I'm breathing fine now. No permanent damage done."

Oliver crouches in front of me and rests his forehead on mine. Closing his eyes, he takes a deep breath. "Are you sure? I couldn't handle it if anything happened to you."

As I sit there, I remember how Oliver has always been like this, so concerned for my well-being and, without thought, I begin to stroke the back of his head to comfort him.

"I'm sure," I whisper. Oliver opens his eyes and is about to say something when the sounds of "Bad Habits" by Ed Sheeran blare from somewhere nearby. My ringtone. My phone, now my nemesis. What bad timing. Oliver jumps up, grabs my phone, and hands it to me before walking away to grab us some towels and giving me some much-needed space.

"Hello?" I answer. It's my mechanic.

"Turns out Frankie is going to make it," I tell Oliver when I hang up the phone. "In fact, she's ready to be picked up now." Oliver glances at me and looks away again as I towel off and wring out my hair.

"That's good news," he's slow to answer. "Do you want me to drive you there to pick her up?"

"No, I'll grab an Uber. Easier for everyone," I add when he looks like he's going to argue.

As I go to leave, I turn and thank Oliver again for all his help over the last twenty-four hours.

"No worries, Lil," he tells me. "Oh, and you may want to put on some more clothes before leaving," he reminds me as I make to leave through the side gate, forgetting my state of undress. "Wouldn't want to be giving any innocent mechanics a heart attack on this fine afternoon."

I laugh at what I think is a joke, though Oliver does not appear to be amused, and head through the sliding back door, towards Amy's room.

"Sorry again for hurting you." Oliver's voice stops me.

"It's really OK," I tell him.

It's a small price to pay for an afternoon spent with Oliver, I think to myself as I leave him behind.

CHAPTER 6

Oliver

A s I watch Lilly walk away, leaving wet footprints in her wake, I sit back down and put my head in my hands. I can't believe I hurt Lilly like that. I close my eyes and can still see the angry red mark from where my foot connected with her chest. Still torn, I think about waking Amy up just to run her through what happened, to get her expert opinion. But I hold off, knowing I need to give myself some breathing space from Lilly and that little bikini. Boy, the image of Lilly in that bikini is going to be burned in my mind forever, along with a catalogue of Lilly looking beautiful and sexy over the years.

This is what I get for taking time out of all the things I had planned for the day and instead spending an hour playing in the swimming pool with Lilly. I should have been working on the presentation that is due on Monday morning, but of course all thoughts of that flew out the window when I saw Lilly in that pink bikini. And that's what Lilly does to me, what she has always done to me. She's a distraction. Bright and colourful, and full of laughter. But a distraction nonetheless. She's also the person who makes me laugh like no one else. I can't help but smile when she's around. But with the amount of power she has always had over me, she tends to leave me feeling unbalanced and unsettled. Feelings I've never been comfortable with.

I think that is what originally drew me to Emma. She's the polar opposite of Lilly. We first met when her firm was doing some legal work for one of our clients, and I felt immediately drawn to how poised she was. She was always so well put together; she seemed so solid. Some would say this isn't a romantic way to think of a partner, but she seemed to fit so well into the life I envisioned for myself. And after years of pining for Lilly, with that moment between us at her last birthday party almost a year ago going ignored, I decided to embrace the predictability of someone like Emma and asked her out. And, if I think back on it, it's been pretty smooth sailing ever since. Granted, we went from newly dating to being like an old married couple in a week, to the point where even I can admit the passion disappeared (if it was ever there to begin with?), but I always knew where I stood with Emma. And where we were going. And I thought that would be enough to keep us together.

Lately, though, I've been feeling dissatisfied with our relationship. Which seems to have coincided in the recent months with a new side of Emma that has suddenly appeared. She now tends to snap at me more often and is frequently rude to the people I love. And when I saw the way she treated Lilly last night, well, that made me angry in a way I don't often get. I'm not prone to big emotions, but when it comes to Lilly, they just come out.

Like, for example, the amount of anxiety I felt upon finding Lilly in that broken-down car last night. Or the fact that I was awake half the night worrying about her alone in that apartment, somehow being protected by a thug with blue hair. It all goes to show that with Lilly, I cannot completely control the way I feel about her, and again, this isn't something I'm altogether comfortable with. My well-ordered life is something I take great pride in. I'm not sure where this inherent need to have everything "just so" came from—my mum often jokes that I came out of the womb already neat and tidy—but I do know that when I'm with Emma, things feel orderly and pleasant. And I guess therein lies the problem. A relationship should feel exciting and passionate, at least some of the time.

So, after dropping Lilly off last night, I did what I knew I had to do. Once I acknowledged that my feelings for Lilly had not in fact disappeared, I attempted to break up with Emma. She did not take it well. She told me to take some time to think about things, that I wasn't acting like myself, that I needed to think about this in a rational way, and only after I pushed back did she agree to "take a break." I guess this is what I get for dating a lawyer. She tried to put together a logical argument for why we work as a couple, when in reality, I don't think we ever worked. Emma was like a dog with a bone though, something I thought I admired in her, so we settled on time apart. She now wants me to spend this time putting together a list of reasons we should break up (she's going to bring a counter argument), and we're going to meet to discuss our future prospects. I can't believe she has given me relationship homework. How has it come to this?

"Hey, Ol, where's Lilly?"

I look up to see Amy walking towards me, a pillow mark indented across her cheek.

"I woke up and all her stuff is gone."

"She went to get her car. The mechanic called, and they were able to fix it. It's ready to be picked up now."

"That's good news," Amy says, giving me a strange look. "Why don't you look happy?"

"I hurt Lilly—"

"Ollie, what did you do to Lilly? Did you say something to upset her?"

As I wonder what I could say to Lilly to upset her, I tell her, "No, I mean, I physically hurt her. We were swimming, and I kicked her, and she got hurt." Just thinking about it again is making my stomach twist into knots. "Can you call her tonight and check on her?"

"Of course, but I'm sure she's fine," Amy tells me with a dismissive wave of her hand. She sits down at the edge of the pool, dangles her feet in the water, and spears me with one of her looks.

"Speaking of getting hurt, what's going on with you and Emma? Is all OK in paradise?" It would seem that the issues between me and Emma are also evident to the people who know me the best.

Not wanting to get into any details with Amy, who has never hidden her dislike of Emma, I give a noncommittal shrug. "It will be fine," is all I offer before changing the subject. "Lilly has popped up quite a bit in the last twenty-four hours. It feels like I've seen her more in the last two days than I have in the last two months."

Amy, never one to sugar coat things, tells it to me straight. "That's because you have a jealous girlfriend who can't handle you being friends with a gorgeous girl like Lilly, so Lilly has stayed away to keep the peace."

I feel a twinge of guilt that my relationship has impeded both my friendship and Amy's friendship with Lilly and vow to do better in the future.

"Well, we won't have to worry about that for too much longer," I tell Amy as I get up and walk back into the house.

"What does that mean?" Amy yells after me, a hint of excitement in her voice.

I avoid answering this, not wanting to spend any more time examining my failed relationship, and instead yell back as I walk into the house, "Don't stay out here too long, Ames! Wouldn't want you to get burned!"

I smile as Amy screeches, "Oliver!" As I walk up the stairs, picking up the wet towel Lilly left hanging over the banister, I think to myself, what am I going to do about you, Lilly?

CHAPTER 7

T HE NEXT MORNING, AS I lie in bed putting off the inevitable start to the day, I think about my encounter in the swimming pool with Oliver. As I poke at the tender bruise I'm now sporting on my chest, I picture the look in his eyes as he touched my chest with gentle hands, and my heart races. Over the years, Oliver and I have had several moments that made my heart hopeful but that all ultimately came to nothing. One particular time comes to mind: almost twelve months ago, a what-if encounter with Oliver, one I try to avoid thinking about altogether.

It was the night of my twenty-third birthday, a week after the disastrous romantic breakup weekend from hell. I had known my now ex-boyfriend Sebastian for a couple of years, through mutual friends, and we had become casual friends ourselves for about six months before he'd asked me out. It had surprised me at first, since I hadn't considered him romantically, but he was persistent, and eventually we started dating in earnest. We had been together for about four months when he convinced me to go away for a romantic weekend with him, and I saw this mini break away together as a positive step forward in our relationship. A private cabin in the snowy mountain tops signified we were getting serious about each other. Unfortunately, Sebastian did not see it this way, and on the second day of the trip, he took the opportunity to break up with me, bruising my heart and shattering my ego. And he did this just before my birthday, the jerk.

And so, the weekend after my birthday, I was not in the mood to go out. However, Amy was having none of this. She convinced me that I had to go out and celebrate my birthday properly or Sebastian would win. She made me get all dressed up, forcing me into a curve-hugging black mini dress (one I had bought on a dare!), plastering my face with make-up, and giving me a sexy hairstyle. With pure determination, she forced me to celebrate my birthday in style. I had given in with some reluctance and only agreed to do it to get her off my case, but also with the caveat that I intended to spend the evening replacing my total blood volume with 100 percent pure vodka.

To my misfortune, Oliver wasn't on board with this plan and insisted on substituting a glass of water for every other drink.

"You will thank me tomorrow," he said, ever the serious person in our group, as he took a vodka shot from my hand and replaced it with a full bottle of water.

"Oliver, I'm fine!" I slurred, looking up at him through bleary eyes. "I need to drink to forget that I'm miserable."

"Why so miserable, Lilly Pad?" he asked, making my drunken heart skip a beat with the use of that particular nickname.

"Because I'm twenty-three and all alone," I moaned.

"OK, grandma. I think you may be being a little dramatic."

"No! I will never find someone to love me!" I declared with a burst of emotion as I placed my heavy head on the table in front of me. "And do you know why I will die alone?" I asked Oliver in my most serious voice while resting my cheek on my hand and beckoning him closer.

Oliver rolled his eyes at my theatrics. "Why, Lilly?"

"Because," I said, urging him even closer so I could whisper straight into his ear, "I'm unlovable."

Oliver stared into my eyes for a moment, his face only inches from mine. "Don't be silly, Lil. You don't mean that."

"I do, 'tis true," I replied, my voice now a little sleepy.

"No," he whispered back. "You are so lovable. Lilly, you are perfect."

As I gaped at Oliver, sure that my beer goggles had been placed over my ears, making them ear goggles, I flashed back to him saying this to me once before—

"Lilly Pilly, wake up!" Amy screeched right next to me, deafening me in one ear. "It's your birthday. Why are you hiding here in a corner with Oliver?"

"Because I'm heartbroken and depressed, remember?"

"Psht, heartbroken? Over that douche? No, I'll not have it. You're young and hot. You're looking smoking tonight. I mean, your boobs are popping in that dress."

I looked down at the not-so-small amount of cleavage I was showing in my dress and had to agree. The girls were looking pretty good tonight. I glanced up to see Oliver was also looking their way, though he blushed and looked away again when he saw I had caught him looking.

"The best way to get over a guy is to get under the next one," Amy declared in an obnoxiously loud voice, laughing at her own joke, making me blush and Oliver's jaw clench.

"Come on, this bar is filled with hot guys. Madi and Sammi are already out on the dance floor. Let's go!" She grabbed my hand and dragged me away with her.

From here, the night picked up. While laughing at Amy's antics, I soon joined in, and the four of us got busy recreating the latest TikTok dances while also downing tequila shots. I gave Oliver a random cheerful wave while he was watching from the sidelines. Towards the latter part of the night, after having said goodbye to Madi and Sammi—the party poopers—I somehow lost Amy before finally spying her flirting with some gorgeous, younger, George Clooney–looking guy at the bar. As I watched in amusement, my best friend chatting with the enthralled stranger, a strong pair of arms wrapped around my waist from behind. Woodsy with a hint of vanilla. Oliver. I sighed as I leaned back into his solid chest. Hmmm, yum.

"Are you OK? Are you having a good night?" he said, his lips close to my ear, making me shiver in delight.

I turned in his arms, linking my arms around his neck. "I would be better if you danced with me on my birthday." Was this my flirting with Oliver?

"Well, don't look now, but it looks like that's what we're doing."

I glanced down to see our bodies pressed together, swaying slowly and out of time to the upbeat version of the Ed Sheeran song "Perfect" thumping in the background. I inched a little closer and closed my eyes, resting my head on his shoulder and sighing. Boy, he smelled so good. How was that possible? I bet I smelled like a vodka brewery—hmmm, was vodka made in a brewery?

Not the time for this, Lilly, I thought to myself. Focus. You are slow dancing with Oliver. It's like a birthday miracle. As I took note of his strong arms—was he pulling me even closer? I felt how soft his skin was under my lips—wait.

Oliver froze against me. "Lilly?"

Did I just kiss Oliver on the neck? Mortified, I raised my eyes to see Oliver looking at me with an intense expression on his face, his gaze bouncing between my eyes and my lips.

"Ollie," I whispered, not wanting to break the spell and ruin the moment. In slow motion, Oliver leaned in, moving ever closer—

"Lilly!" My arm got jerked away in a sudden motion. "We have to leave! Now!" Amy hissed, dragging me away from Oliver. "I think I just tried to hit on my new co-worker."

"What?" I asked, bewildered, still looking back to where Oliver remained, watching me with that intense look. "What did you say?"

"The new doctor starting at the emergency department? That's him. The delicious snack over there. And I was flirting with him. We have to leave; I need to find a new job…" Amy continued to rant as we moved closer to the door. "Hurry up, Lil!"

"Lilly?" Oliver's voice stopped me in my tracks. I turned to see him looking at me with an expression I could not decipher. As he looked at me, he swallowed hard and asked in a hoarse voice, "Do you guys need a ride home?"

"Ollie, we have an Uber waiting outside. You stay and have fun," Amy answered for both of us, grabbing my coat and shoving me out the door.

And that was that. The night we almost kissed. We have never spoken of it since, never even hinted at it. The next morning, I woke up alternating between slight cringing and full-scale mortification. Every time I recalled kissing Oliver on the neck, I shrank into my body a bit and my skin crawled with embarrassment. In the weeks that followed the incident, I avoided the Harlow household, only seeing Amy out or at my place, and after about three weeks, Oliver started dating Emma, and they've been together ever since, close to ten months now. From this, I concluded that Oliver either did not remember or did not care too much about the incident and that in his mind, it was a mistake, one best never mentioned, or better still, best forgotten.

And now I groan as I force myself out of bed, needing to get on with my day. I have to do my laundry, clean my bathroom, and pay some bills. All the things adults do. And all tasks that seem dull, so I decide to whip up a batch of blueberry mini muffins instead while at the same time researching pop-up cafés. As I'm scrolling through my favourite Pinterest pages, a text comes through from Oliver.

OLIVER: Lilly?

LILLY: New phone, who dis?

OLIVER: Oh sorry, I thought this was Lilly's phone number?

Gosh, he behaves like an old man sometimes!

LILLY: Yes, grandpa. It's me.

OLIVER: Can't even text like a normal person, hey?

I smile.

LILLY: Hello, Oliver. What can I do for you today?

OLIVER: Smart arse.

OLIVER: I have an idea for your business, your café/bakery idea.

Oh? I glance down to see if I'm presentable, shrugging, thinking of how I presented myself to Oliver yesterday, and then press the video call function and get the pleasure of seeing Oliver's face fill my mobile phone screen. Why don't I do this more often?

"Hi, Lil, how's your chest?" he asks straightaway.

"All reviews on the matter are pretty positive. I've had no complaints," I say in jest, watching him blush.

He clears his throat. "I mean your bruise. Are you OK?"

"I'm fine," I insist. "Now tell me about this idea you have."

"Have you heard about the Market Place, down at Federation Square?" he asks. "They have a market there every Sunday." When I shake my head, he goes on to describe the market where local small business owners can run stalls, showcasing samples of their products to test the quality of them and the public's interest in them while making some money along the way.

"I think it would be the perfect opportunity to get you out there, see what it's like to run a stall before committing to something more," he concludes.

"Oh my gosh!" I exclaim. "That sounds perfect!"

"Great, because I called them this morning and reserved a booth for you for next Sunday."

"Next Sunday?" I cry. "That soon?" I don't work on the weekend, so that isn't a factor. It's just that shouldn't I need more than a week to get something of this magnitude together?

"You will be fine, Lil. Just put together a few of your favourite recipes and see how they're received. Amy and I can help you on the day."

"Really? That would be amazing. Thank you, Oliver."

"You're welcome." He smiles at me, his eyes crinkling in their adorable way. "I'll email you the details later so you can get started planning." He hesitates. "Do you need help with your plan?"

Boy, he must think I'm incompetent. I will show him, I think with a surge of confidence.

"No, Oliver. I can handle a few ideas on a piece of paper," I reply, my voice as dry as sandpaper, but then, unable to stop myself, I smile back at him. "I'm so excited!"

"Great, well, I'm going to go now. I've got some work to do."

"Of course you do," I tell him, giving a little wave goodbye. Oliver always seems to have work to do.

As Oliver hangs up and the screen goes black, I let out a big breath. I may not be getting any closer to marking number four off my list—getting over Oliver, that is—but I'm determined to make at least some of my New Year's resolutions a reality, and this market stall is bringing me one step closer to numbers one and two. Opening my own café and quitting my job are tangible things for me now. And as an email from Oliver comes through confirming all the logistical details, I get to work on sorting out my favourite recipes. This is going to be great.

CHAPTER 8

Lilly

MONDAY MORNING HAS ME CRASHING back down to earth. After an eventful weekend filled with lovely moments with Oliver and solid plans to make my Love, Lilly café a one-day-soon reality, to be sitting here answering mundane phone calls and avoiding leering glances is so depressing.

"Lilly, have you sent through that contract to Mrs Peterson?" my boss, aka public enemy number one, asks me not for the first time this morning. He stops at my desk and stares at my chest.

"Yes, Mr Hall. I sent it through this morning, like you asked me to." In my mind, I call him my special nickname for him, Toad Face (like Toad Hall from The Wind and the Willows), and it gives me a secret thrill each time. And he also looks like a toad, so my pun works on so many levels.

"Great, good," he says, still staring at my body. I glance down at the unflattering shirt that I'm wearing and wonder what he could be so fascinated by. I go out of my way to look as frumpy as possible at work, and it just doesn't seem to make any of them keep their eyes, or their hands, to themselves.

"So, Lilly, got yourself a boyfriend yet?" he asks. So inappropriate.

"That's not something I want to talk about at work, Mr Hall. As you know, I'm very focused on my career when I'm here," I say not for the first time.

"Good, good. You should be focused on the work you're doing here," he says. The man is so oblivious to the disgust I'm aiming his way. "We love having you here to decorate the place."

Oh, gross. Could this guy get any more sexist? I bite my tongue to avoid saying something I may regret later and smile at him through gritted teeth.

"Your twelve o'clock appointment should be here soon. Don't you need to get prepared?" I ask, trying to get rid of him.

"Of course, yes. Good to chat to you as always, Lilly," he says with one last glance at my breasts as he strolls away, without an awareness of the daggers I'm shooting at his back.

"Ribbit," I croak at him, under my breath.

I pull up the girls' group chat and send a message: I hate it here. Must quit.

Madi doesn't reply because she has a job as a sales rep that keeps her busy during the day.

Sammi sends a meme from The Office, with Pam saying "yup." (Sammi loves a good GIF or emoji and does not like to text in full sentences.)

AMY: *Do it! You can find another job. One where you aren't sexually harassed daily.*

Sammi sends a thumbs-up emoji.

LILLY: *I just need to last a little while longer until I can get my business going. Sunday's market will be a good start.*

AMY: I know. I just hate that you're stuck there.

SAMMI: Me too :(

LILLY: Me too :(

AMY: Shall we all meet for lunch tomorrow?

Sammi sends another thumbs-up emoji.

LILLY: Yes! Can't wait!

AMY: Got to go. Hot shot doc is demanding my presence by his side. Love you.

Sammi says goodbye via a waving emoji.

I smile at the thought of Amy going at it with Dr McHottie and, with a sigh, get back to the mountain of paperwork in front of me.

As the day drags on, I find time to work on my list of baked goods for the market stall on Sunday. I add both Amy's and Oliver's favourite cookies, of course, knowing that Madi and Sammi love them too. Along with my signature blueberry-and-coconut mini muffins, the classic banana-and-walnut bread, and the double chocolate fudge brownies that are always a crowd pleaser. I start putting together an ingredient list when it hits me. How am I going to bake this amount of food in my kitchen, which is the size of a postage stamp?

In times like this in the past, I would have used my parents' kitchen for a big-scale bake, but a few months ago, they moved about an hour's flight away so that my dad could accept a position as professor of microbiology at some fancy university in Sydney. I'm so proud of his achievement. After toiling away in academia for most of his life, it was a wonderful reward to be given such a prestigious position.

When I was growing up, I always felt a slight disconnect from my quiet, serious, academic parents. Although I always felt loved and cared for, I'm not sure I always felt accepted. I arrived in a blur of colour into their lives later than they had expected, perhaps an accident after many childless years, and they didn't quite know how to handle a child with such big emotions and with smaller academic prowess. It is clear that they support me as best they can, though they never embraced my love of baking and both pushed me into getting a basic bachelor's degree, as they think any university degree is better than none. In my quiet moments, I didn't agree with this, but being a people pleaser, I struggled through the three-year course, and when I graduated and ended up in a dead-end position as a secretary, despite having said university degree under my belt, I couldn't help but feel I was a disappointment to them.

Often when they call to ask me about my life, their questions come with a side of judgment. When are you going to get a better job? Is there anything we can do to help you get a better job? Maybe Amy can help you get a better job? Boy, do they love Amy. Amy, the bookworm who loves to study and aced all her exams. Whenever she came to visit us, they would light up as she spoke about her biology and physiology classes, in a way they never did when I discussed the science behind a perfectly made croissant. So, when they moved away, while I felt sad at their everyday absence in my life, I also felt a sense of relief that they had taken the weight of their unmet expectations along with them.

LILLY: Amy, can I use your kitchen this Saturday to make a mountain of mess, I mean, treats? :)

AMY: Sure, fine with me. But best to check with Oliver, make sure he doesn't have any plans to use the kitchen (unlikely).

LILLY: Will do, thanks, A.

AMY: :)

I pull up my chat thread with Oliver and type, Oliver?
His reply is immediate: What do you need?
I smile because he knows me too well.

LILLY: Why do you think I need something? Maybe I just want to say hi?

OLIVER: I'm waiting...

LILLY: OK, well, I may need a tiny favour...

OLIVER: ...

LILLY: Is it OK if I borrow your kitchen on Saturday? To bake for the Sunday market. You know, the one you signed me up for? So you kind of need to say yes...

OLIVER: Of course you can use the kitchen. It's not like Ames or I use it very much.

This is true. The Harlow siblings are more inclined to use the kitchen to store their takeout leftovers than to create any culinary masterpieces. A shame, really.

OLIVER: Will I need to organise an industrial cleaner to come on Saturday night? :)

LILLY: Ha ha, I'm not that bad.

OLIVER: ...

LILLY: Well, maybe just have the fire department on speed dial, just in case.

I text this back to him, referencing a small explosion that happened when I tried to roast marshmallows in the toaster. The fire and police departments responded to what they had thought was a bomb going off. It was mortifying to have to explain it was just a small kitchen mishap. I was only twelve at the time, for goodness' sake, but it's not something one ever lives down.

OLIVER: *Come over any time. Either Amy or I'll be there to let you in.*

LILLY: *Thanks, Ol. See you then.*

OLIVER: *xx*

Two kisses? I'm tempted to send back a bunch of kisses of my own, but as an image of Emma pops into my head, I force myself to put my phone away. Kisses from Oliver to me are done with friendly affection, but my return kisses would have a whole different meaning.

The rest of the week goes by both at a slow pace (office hours) and at speed (any time I'm preparing for Sunday). I meet Amy and Sammi for lunch on Thursday (we FaceTime Madi into the catch up as she sits in the airport lounge, waiting to board a plan for some fancy conference somewhere), during which we discuss the upcoming Market Place stall, with the three of us playing with menu ideas and what we think would be the best crowd pleasers. I show them what I've mapped out, and they all agree that these are in fact their favourite Love, Lilly treats and therefore must be on the menu.

With this settled, Amy starts ranting about Dr McHottie and how he has found a new way to irritate her this week.

"So we had this new nurse start in our department last week, and he's gorgeous!" she tells us while we brace ourselves for what this could mean. "And I think he wanted to ask me out. We were flirting, and then all of a sudden, bam! Dr Douche has taken him away from me, just had him transferred to another department. I didn't even know he had the power to do that to nurses."

Sami and I look at each other, smiling behind our hands, and Amy, upon seeing this, launches a handful of French fries at our heads.

"It's not funny, guys. It's infuriating. There's not a single part of my life that this man hasn't tried to infiltrate. First my job and now my love life."

"You seem to be getting very worked up about this," I tell her in a soothing tone, fearing another fry to the head.

"And it's not like he has moved this nurse man to the moon," Sammi adds, ever the practical one. "You can still find him and ask him out."

"As per usual, you guys appear to be missing the point. It's the principle of the matter. You'd be furious too if you had someone like this in your life meddling and messing with things."

I remember back to how good looking this guy is and don't 100 percent agree with this assessment. But I also don't want to upset Amy any further, so as always, I'm on her side.

"Absolutely, Ames. The guy is a jerk. Let's just hope he will move to another hospital soon and you will be rid of him. They do that on Grey's Anatomy a lot, you know? Move hospitals," I finish, filled with knowledge on the matter.

Sammi nods at this. "Yup, Derek moved all the way to Boston in season eleven. Maybe your McHottie will do that too?"

"You two and your Grey's Anatomy," Amy laughs at us, seeming to snap out of her dark mood. "You know that it doesn't work like that in real life? But maybe you're right. He may move to another department soon, and then he will finally be out of my hair."

We both nod in solidarity as I think to myself that perhaps she's protesting too much and that maybe she has a crush. But I also keep this to myself. If Amy isn't ready to face her true feelings, who am I to rush her?

After this soul-refreshing girls' lunch, and in the lead-up to the Sunday market stall, I also have the pleasure of texting back and forth with Oliver. Although he often speaks about how busy work is for him at the moment, he still has found the time to bounce about a few marketing and brand strategies for Love, Lilly with me, including a gorgeous logo that he somehow found the time to design.

For my part, I've been sending him annoying links to cat videos and clips of goats screaming. So, you know, we're both dedicated and working hard to make my dreams a reality. And as the weekend approaches, I'm filled with anticipation for what could just be the start of my big career break.

CHAPTER 9

Lilly

S ATURDAY MORNING ARRIVES, AND I'M puffed up with confidence and three arm loads of ingredients. With the help of my pal Johnny, who seems pretty excited about my upcoming market stall, promising to come down and visit if he can, I load Frankie with all the products a person could need to create every sugary treat imaginable. I tuck my trusty laptop into my bag, and I hop into the driver's seat. I wanted to print and laminate all my recipes before today, but the bean counters at O'Brien/O'Ryan take note of every page printed at the office, and I don't want to risk getting fired so close to being able to quit.

As I drive to the Harlow house, I make a mental plan on how I'm going to tackle the day ahead. I'm planning on baking two dozen double chocolate chip cookies with M&M'S, two dozen chocolate mint cookies, a dozen blueberry mini muffins, two ba-nana-and-walnut loaves, and two trays of my double chocolate fudge brownies. Everything has to go just right for me today to get this all done on time.

As I pull up to the driveway, I see Oliver out front, getting ready to leave for his run. Damn, that boy likes to be active.

He jogs up to my car when he catches sight of me. "Hey, Lilly, need a hand bringing in stuff from your car?"

I tear my eyes away from his tight running top, hugging his shoulders nice and snug, and smile. "Thanks, Ol. That'd be a great help."

It takes two trips to get all the groceries into the kitchen as Oliver laughs, "Did you leave any sugar on the shelves at the store, Lilly?"

I glance around at what is six kilos of sugar in various varieties and reflect that maybe it does look excessive, but I had all my calculations made and I'm certain this is the right amount.

"OK, I'm going to go for my run now," Oliver says once I've unpacked the last of the bags onto the counter. Before he leaves, he hesitates as he looks around at what already looks like chaos. Organised chaos is how I see it. "Unless you need me to stay and help? Amy is out all day, but I can lend a hand if you need?"

"I'll be fine." I give him a little push towards the door. "Don't you worry about a thing."

Oliver looks at me, his eyes filled with doubt, my track record of past disasters working against me, and says, "The fire extinguisher is in the hallway, just in case." And with that, he runs out the front door.

"Smart arse," I mutter to myself as I check to see that there is in fact a fire extinguisher sitting in plain view. "Humph, I'll show him."

I get to work measuring out ingredients and melting butter. I have one stand mixer stirring the cookie dough and another creaming together some butter and sugar. I'm a well-oiled baking machine. As I get into a groove, things start to come together, and before I know it, I have two batches of cookies in the oven.

"Off to a great start, Lilly," I congratulate myself. And then right on cue, things take a turn for the worse. All of a sudden, I have too many things going on at once. There are three pans of various chocolate types melting on the stove, a stand mixer whirring out of control on the counter, and two timers going off at the same time. What are these timers even for? And then, the smoke alarm goes off.

"Lilly?" Oliver yells, running into the room with the fire extinguisher ready to go. "What's happening?"

I turn to see my roasted hazelnuts burning to a crisp on the stove, sending up plumes of smoke, and groan. As Oliver goes to open the windows to let out the smoke, and let some fresh air in, I wave a tea towel under the smoke alarm in a feeble attempt to silence it.

When the blaring of the alarm comes to a sudden halt, I take stock of my current situation. Burned nuts on the frying pan, melted chocolate spilling over onto the stove, and dishes upon dishes piled high on every surface. Why did I think I could do this?

I sit at the counter and put my head in my hands. This is, as most would have predicted, an unmitigated disaster.

"Hey, Lilly. It's OK," Oliver says from beside me, stroking my back. "You can do this."

"I'd say that the evidence is pointing to the contrary." I gesture to the mess in front of us.

"You just need a system," he says as another timer goes off. For what, I have no idea. I look at him with doubt as he asks, "Where are your recipes?"

"I have them on my laptop." I point to where it sits, covered in some sort of sticky substance. "I have a spreadsheet and everything to keep track of what I need to do."

"OK, let me have a look," he says as he wakes up my computer. On the home screen in front of him is a photo of the three of us— me, Oliver, and Amy—taken at my birthday bash last year. It was snapped before the vodka had taken hold of me and my decision-making abilities, and it's a favourite of mine. Oliver gives the picture a close look and then glances at me, the muscle in his cheek twitching.

"So what am I looking for?" he asks.

I pull the laptop over to me and, in a quick motion, open up the Excel spreadsheet to cover the photo in an attempt to put aside any memories of that night. "See? I made a spreadsheet with all the ingredients in this tab and times for baking, mixing, stirring in this one. It's all very organised," I say, filled with pride, as another timer goes off. A fourth one?

Oliver smiles at me, also maybe a little proud at my attempt to have a system in place?

He gets up. "I know what you need to get through today," he says. "Me." I blink at him, unsure of where he's going with this.

"Let me be your sous chef," he adds, grabbing an apron and going to wash his hands. "Between the two of us, we'll get this in order."

As I watch, he takes a tray of cookies out of the oven and, with expert hands, puts them on the cooling rack.

"Come on, Lilly. No time to waste. Turn that stand mixer off and figure out what that timer is for," he says as another timer goes off. How many timers did I set?

For the next three hours, Oliver and I work side by side, following my well-designed spreadsheet—see, I knew it would work—and with some luck, things start to come together. As we work, we talk about everything and anything. Oliver tells me about how his boss is thinking of retiring soon and that he may be next in line for another promotion. He confides in me that although this is what he has been working so hard for, now that it's becoming a reality, he's unsure whether he wants to take it, based on how many hours they already expect him to work. This perspective from Oliver is surprising for me, given how he has always been single-mindedly ambitious. I never expected for him to get to his goal and not want to grab it with both hands. Maybe Oliver is changing?

In return, I tell him about the crazy cleaning lady at work who doesn't think young women should be single and have careers and who leaves me "Jesus loves you" pamphlets on my desk every morning. As I tell him this, Oliver gives me an incredulous look and then bursts out laughing.

"These things could only happen to you, Lilly. What does she think you do at work, anyway?"

"I have no idea," I reply. "She just knows I'm one of only two women at the office and maybe assumes the worst." Oliver goes to say something, perhaps in reference to the terrible male-to-female ratio at my workplace, when the oven timer goes off.

"Last one!" I say as I pull the final batch of mini muffins from the oven.

After taking two muffins off the cooling rack, I follow Oliver to the couch, sinking into it with a groan. I was standing for hours, and it feels amazing to get off my feet. As I turn and see Oliver sitting on the other end of the couch, I smile and pass him a muffin.

"For your troubles," I say, my heart singing with gratitude for his help today.

Oliver bites into the warm muffin with vigour and sighs. "These really are the best muffins, Lilly. I know I just helped you bake them, but I don't understand what makes them so amazing."

I smile at him, and with the of air of someone filled with mischief, I whisper, "I added heroin to them when you weren't looking."

Oliver chokes on his mouthful as I let out a loud laugh. He throws a cushion at my head. "You brat!" he says, finishing his "drug-laced" confection.

"Thanks again for your help today. I wouldn't have been able to get that done without you."

"You would have figured it out," he replies. "But I'm glad I could help. And happy to keep my house from burning down," he adds with a grin.

"And you say I'm a brat." I throw a cushion back at him and lean my head against the couch with a sigh.

"Oh crap, I'm going to be late," Oliver says, checking his watch and jumping up, wiping his hands on his running shorts. "I promised I'd take Emma out for an early dinner. We need to talk about a few things, and it's almost 5:30. I have to grab a shower and get going," he adds as he rushes towards the door, muttering something about homework and lists. They have a bizarre relationship.

"Five thirty dinner, what are you? Senior citizens?" I ask, feeling sad that he has to go.

"Emma has a virtual meeting with clients in Hong Kong later tonight, so this is the only chance we can see each other today," he tells me, inadvertently making me feel small by making Emma seem important.

"OK, have fun. I'll just finish up here." I wave towards the kitchen. "And then I'll head home. See you tomorrow?"

"Yes, I'll be there bright and early." He heads towards the bathroom. "Don't forget to set your alarm clock for the morning!" he yells over his shoulder.

"Alarm clock, he reminds me," I mutter to myself after Oliver has left the room. "Like I'm some incompetent, forgetful child." I huff to myself before conceding that sleeping in and missing the market altogether does sound like something I'd do.

Oliver rushes out of the house fifteen minutes later, with what looks like a manila folder tucked under his arm, yelling goodbye as he runs out of the door. I lie back down on the couch and close my eyes. It's been a very long day, and now I have trays upon trays of baked goods to pack away into airtight containers, ready for the trip home. Maybe if I close my eyes just for a minute, I will find the energy to get moving.

The next thing I notice is someone placing a warm blanket on me and taking off my shoes. I snuggle down deeper into sleep and mumble, "Thanks," to the helpful stranger who is making me more comfortable. As I fall back deeper into sleep, I feel a soft kiss on my forehead, followed by a gruff voice saying, "Night, Lilly."

CHAPTER 10

I WAKE THE NEXT DAY to sunlight streaming onto my face and a sore neck. Where am I? With some trouble, I sit up, wincing as I straighten my spine and look around. Am I still on the Harlows' couch? Did I really sleep, like, fourteen hours last night? Wait! That means it's market day, and I've left all my market stall food out on the bench all night.

"No!" I groan as I get to my feet, noticing I must have kicked off my shoes at some point and somehow found myself a blanket? Everything will be stale or soggy, having been left out all night.

"Good job, Lil," I tell myself as I limp to the kitchen. "Way to mess up your first trial run." As I enter the kitchen, I rub my tired eyes, trying to make sense of all the neatly packed away cookies and muffins on the counter and the brownies in the fridge where they belong. Hmm? How did this happen? I think back to last night, Oliver rushing out to see Emma, my procrastinating cleaning up with a power nap that raged out of control, a kiss on the forehead—wait. Was that a dream? Oliver must have come home, seen me passed out on the couch—please god, not snoring or drooling—and come to my rescue, again. As much as it bothers me to always be in his debt, I do owe him for this one.

I look at the time and see that I need to get home and get ready to make it to the market on time, so I leave a note to my hero, thanking him yet again for saving the day, and gathering up my stuff, I rush out the door. Once home, I hurry through a shower, washing my hair and plaiting it in a big braid, Lara Croft–style, to keep it out of the way. Now on to my outfit. What does a successful business-type woman wear to her opening event? In the blistering heat? I settle for a fitted black T-shirt tucked into high-waisted shorts, paired with Roman sandals tied in a criss-cross pattern up my legs, stopping mid-calf. There! Comfortable, stylish, and sweat resistant. I glance at the time and start loading up my car again, waving goodbye to the ever-present Johnny, excited to be on my way.

When I get to the market, having had to park miles down the road because of the busy nature of the event, I look around for the stall Oliver reserved for me. Number 132. As I crane my neck to look at the stall numbers around me, balancing my trays and Tupperware containers precariously in my arms, I see Oliver up ahead. And he's putting up a sign, a sign with the Love, Lilly logo he crafted last week, the one I raved about. He had it printed for me? I rush up to the trestle table, dumping my stuff, and grab Oliver.

"When did you do this?" I ask.

He turns and, as he so often does, runs his eyes over me, pausing on my long braid and sandals with a smile.

"You can't launch your business without identifying your brand, Lil," he replies like a true marketer. "You must have a logo that people can recognise and search for."

I squeal as I look at it again and pull him into a hug, this one going for thirteen seconds as we both appear happy to stay in each other's arms.

"Ahem," Amy says from somewhere behind me. "I'm here too and very early for a Sunday morning, might I add." With a lot of reluctance, I pull away from Oliver and see my best friend grinning at me, looking adorable in her short denim overalls.

"I see that, Ames, and I'm ever so grateful."

"You're welcome. Now let's get this set up before your hordes of customers arrive."

As we lay out the treasures baked with love the day before, Oliver fusses over the sign, "aiming for maximum visibility," he informs us. Once everything is set up, I turn to see a few people waiting in line and get to work.

"What can I get for you?" I ask the first customers, an older lady with her two teenage sons by her side.

"We'll take two cookies, a slice of banana bread, and a brownie, please." The older lady pulls out her wallet. As I attend to this, my first ever sale, Oliver is taking photos, again fixing the logo until it's just right.

"Did you see that, guys?" I ask as my customers walk away, munching on their treats with enjoyment. "I sold something! If nothing else comes from today, I made one sale."

"Well, don't look now," Amy replies, "but you're about to make some more." I look to see a queue forming in front of the stall and leap into action. Amy, god bless her, jumps in to help too, and before long, we've sold out of almost half my stock. My stall has had a constant stream of customers, including the very excited Madi and Sammi, both purchasing a lot and demanding I take selfies with them to post on their socials. And of course Johnny also made a visit, though with him in line, the queue shrank in size somewhat. Maybe he's scarier to look at than I think.

"I should have made more," I tell Amy as I wipe some sweat off my forehead when we finally hit a lull. Where have all these people come from?

"Your booth is a featured post on the Market Place Instagram page," a young man says to me from the booth next door. "So people who log on to see what's happening at the market see your booth first. It's smart marketing. Wish I had thought of it," he adds as he turns away to serve a customer. Wish I had thought of it too, I think as I turn to see Oliver messing about on his phone, playing with filters for some of the photos he took earlier.

"Oliver? Did you organise to have my Love, Lilly stand featured on the Market Place Instagram account?"

Oliver looks a little sheepish. "I hope I didn't overstep my bounds. But it just makes the best sense from a marketing perspective. You don't want to be just one of the many stalls here. You want to be the stall that everyone is talking about."

"But, Ollie, what if I hadn't been able to get it all together for today? What if you hadn't stepped in to save the day and I had left all the stuff out on the bench last night, rendering them all inedible? Then you would have featured a stall on Instagram with no food!"

"I knew that wouldn't happen, Lil," he says. "I knew you'd be amazing today, and look! You've almost sold out of all the cookies and brownies. People are raving about your food online." He takes his phone and shows me the comment section from the Love, Lilly Instagram post.

"A taste of heaven," I read one comment out loud.

"These cookies are to die for. I hope this stall is here next week. Can I buy them anywhere else?" another comment says. I look up at Oliver, a little dazed.

"They're all positive," I say in wonder.

"Yes, Lilly, they are," Oliver replies, grinning at me, his smiling gaze running over my face. "You have a successful business soft launch here today."

As I continue to scroll through the comments section of Instagram, I take in both Oliver and Amy manning the booth and working so hard to make this a success for me. My eyes fill with tears as I look at the only family I have nearby, forever grateful that Amy chose my sandwich to steal almost twenty years ago.

"No tears today," Amy states as she pulls me into a side hug. "Today is a good day."

"These are happy tears," I say, rushing to reassure them as Oliver looks on with concern. "I'm so grateful to you both. How can I ever repay you?"

"By letting us sample the merchandise," Amy quips as she grabs a mini muffin. "I'm going to get us some fresh lemonade from that stall over there. Have you seen the guy squeezing the lemons? Be still my heart," Amy says as she makes her way over to the juice stand.

"So, Lilly," Oliver grabs my attention again. "You need to create a Love, Lilly Instagram page and start posting pictures of your food on there. Get people drooling over the photos. You could even post videos of you baking. I know that will provide some amusing content," he adds with a smirk. I'm sure he's thinking back on the scene he came home to yesterday afternoon.

"Not every baking session is that chaotic, I will have you know," I tell him with a wink. "Can you send me some of the photos you took today? I'll add them as my first post."

As Oliver sends me some pictures, I serve the next batch of customers and hear the all-too-familiar voice of Emma in the distance. That can't be right, can it? She wouldn't be here to lend her support.

"Hi, Lucy, cute stall you have here," Emma says as she steps up to Oliver and kisses him on the cheek.

"Hey," Oliver says, frowning and pulling away from her slightly. "What are you doing here?"

"I came to see you, of course. We didn't have time to finish our presentations last week"—presentations?—"and our date last Friday was interrupted when you had to help Lilly get home after she let her car break down," she adds, giving me a pointed look. Oliver looks at her, confused and a little weary.

"Sorry again about that, Emma," I say as sincerely as possible, knowing Oliver hates when Amy and I put him in the middle of our war with Emma. Trying to be the bigger person, I offer Emma a choice of the remaining treats. "On the house," I say.

"Oh, I just couldn't eat that much refined sugar." She runs her hand over her perfectly flat stomach. "That number of carbohydrates turns straight into cellulite," she adds, looking at my thighs with a mean smile.

I flush, feeling embarrassed and small, as I often do in Emma's presence, and now overweight and lumpy as well? As I back away and start fiddling with the cake stand, Oliver says, frowning at Emma, "You don't need to worry about any of that, Lil." I muster up a weak smile for him and serve the next customer, grateful to have something to do to keep me busy. If I stop to think too much about what Emma just implied, I'll embarrass myself by crying. Overall, I know I have a decent body—nice, even. My boobs are perky, my hips slightly rounded (and that's the fashion these days, isn't it?), but when I compare myself to the tall, lean, almost fragile frame of Oliver's girlfriend, I feel like a small, round frump.

When I glance up again, Oliver and Emma have walked away looking like they're in a heated discussion, and Amy has returned with two tall glasses of iced lemonade and lemonade guy's phone number.

"What's wrong?" she asks, taking in my expression.

"Nothing," I say, not wanting to get into the Emma situation with her again and end up causing more problems for Oliver. If Amy knew what Emma said to me, she would pounce on Emma like a lioness on a helpless gazelle.

"Just thirsty," I add, taking a big drink. "So you got lemonade guy's phone number? He's cute!"

Amy smiles but without enthusiasm. "Yeah, he is. And he's keen to get together, so maybe I will call him?"

"You should definitely call him. Why wouldn't you?"

"No, I will. Definitely. I'll definitely call him," Amy declares, like she's trying to convince herself this is the truth.

Before I can probe her reluctance to contact the cute man any further, Oliver returns sans Emma but now accompanied by someone else who looks familiar, one of Oliver's friends I've met a few times in passing. What's his name? David? Dan?

"Hey, guys, you remember my friend from work, Dale?" That's it, Dale! "Dale, this is my sister, Amy. And this is Lilly."

"Hi, Dale," Amy and I chorus together.

Dale gives us a big, open smile, zeroing in on me with a curious look on his face. "I've heard a lot about you. Looks like you've got some amazing food here."

Dale takes a step up to the stall and starts asking questions about the cookies and brownies and if I come to this marketplace often. With his attention focused on me, I feel my face flush. Is he flirting with me?

"So, Lilly, are you seeing anyone at the moment?" Dale asks. He is flirting with me!

I look at Oliver and Amy, who are both watching on with interest, Oliver's cheek flexing in and out, and reply almost shyly, "Not at the moment."

Dale grins at this. "Maybe we can get together sometime?"

I feel so thrown by this sudden turn of events that I look at Amy with pleading eyes, begging her to help me out. It's not that I don't think Dale is cute, but there's no way I could fathom dating one of Oliver's friends.

"Lilly, I think you have some customers to serve," Amy says, being a loyal friend and providing me with a distraction.

"Oh yes, thanks, Ames." I turn to see a line of customers waiting to be served, and I manage to bypass Dale's question with a quick, "It was nice to meet you."

From the corner of my eye, I see a grumpy-looking Oliver drag Dale away, the two of them nudging each other in a manly way. What was that all about?

"So we're almost done here," Amy says after we've served the next round of customers, looking around at the near empty table in front of us, beaming in delight. "You did it!"

"We did it!" I remind her. "You, me, and especially Oliver. I can't believe he put so much effort into this for me."

"Can't you?" Amy asks with a strange expression on her face. "You know Oliver would do anything for you."

And with that lovely thought in mind, I start packing up my stall, basking in the glow of my first day as a business owner and baker extraordinaire.

CHAPTER 11

Lilly

T HAT NIGHT, AS I SIT on the couch, rubbing my tired feet, I reflect on what a success the day was. Earlier, when I added up the amount I made today, considering the money I spent on ingredients, it turned out I had made a tidy profit, and I couldn't be more pleased with myself. Maybe I could make this dream a reality. Remembering Oliver's instructions to set up a Love, Lilly Instagram page, so my new fanbase can find me and hopefully my pop-up café in the future, I pull my laptop over to me, unable and unwilling to move even a little bit off the couch, and open the Instagram app. I get to work creating a new account, adding the logo Oliver designed and sent through to me earlier as the profile picture for the page, and also a brief description of what the business is about. After this is done, I pause to decide what my first post should be, and I scroll through the pictures Oliver sent through to choose the perfect picture, stopping on one that catches my eye. It's from the start of the day, which is why I don't look like a hot mess yet. I'm holding a tray of cookies and smiling at the camera / Oliver, the photographer. The cookies look amazing, and I look happy. I decide this will be my first post, with the caption, "Made with love." I add a bunch of what I think are relevant hashtags and remember to tag the Market Place Instagram page in my post to encourage anyone who visited my stall today to follow my account. Feeling pretty impressed with my social media skills, I close the app, content to leave it at this for now.

With my baking business done for the moment, I continue to scroll through the pictures from the day and am forced to think about the encounter with Emma. Why does she have to be so snide all the time? Would it kill her to just pretend to like me, like I do with her? I need a drink to take the edge off my sore body and hurt feelings and limp into the kitchen to make myself a Long Island Iced Tea. OK, well maybe not quite a Long Island Iced Tea, more like adding all the alcohol I have in my apartment into a glass with a splash of coke and a straw. Fancy. I settle back onto the couch with my cocktail, which FYI, does not taste nice but is giving me a warm buzz, and flip on the TV, scrolling through Netflix. Unable to find something good to watch among the several thousand shows available, and feeling unsettled, I turn the TV on mute and try to put my finger on what's bothering me. I should be happy. Today was a good day. And yet I can't revel in any genuine happiness.

The conversation with Dale has also left me feeling uneasy. Given that I had already met him, albeit briefly, in the past and he wasn't flirtatious with me before, the entire experience was odd. And it has left me feeling a bit off kilter, especially seeing Oliver's reaction to it. It was almost like he was jealous, but that can't be right, can it? Surely, given that Oliver is coupled up with Emma, he should be fine with me dating one of his friends. Not that I'd go out with Dale. Although he is very cute, it would just be too weird, given the lingering feelings I have for Oliver. It's all so confusing.

I take another sip of my not-so-fancy drink, grimacing at the taste, and glance at the table. I see my New Year's resolution to-do list and can finally identify why the events of the day have left me feeling so unsettled. Between Oliver's girlfriend and Oliver's flirty friend, I'm left with the fact that I'm nowhere near being able to check off item number four. While I'm going full steam ahead with my grand plans to quit my job and start my business, I'm falling even further behind in my quest to get over this crush.

With another sip of my "Long Island Iced Tea," which perhaps, now that I think of it, does taste nice, I decide to make myself another one, taking this time to consider my options. Oliver is unavailable. He's with the evil Emma, and while not seeming happy all the time, he is committed. And even if he were to become single, I don't think he would ever be interested in someone like me. So I must do something about it. I sway on my feet as I sink onto the couch, holding my cocktail like it's my lifeline. I grab my laptop again and open up a popular dating site, one Amy swears by. If the idea of dating Dale feels wrong, maybe it will feel right to date someone new, someone I've never even met yet. Maybe my person is just out there on the World Wide Web, waiting for me. I create a new profile, choosing the picture from my one and only Instagram post, and add a brief description of myself, making sure to highlight that I am an entrepreneur and business owner. Once I complete this to my satisfaction, I scroll through the many potential suitor accounts listed, looking for my soul mate, hoping he will present himself to me through some sort of divine intervention. Instead, there just seems to be many men with pictures of themselves holding freshly caught fish (what's that about?), lots of photos of shirtless men at the gym (seriously?), and a few men who think photos of them with their mothers is a good look. Dear me, these are some slim pickings. I slurp on my drink, feeling more than a little tipsy and cognitively impaired, and soldier on, determined to make a match or two before the night's end.

Half an hour later—and many, many unfortunate profiles rejected—I stop at a picture that catches my eye. The profile name is "Man with Dog," which isn't terrible. He's also quite cute. Brown hair, brown eyes, dimples. And in his picture, he has his shirt on, with no fish or mother in sight. He is also cuddling a very cute puppy, so bonus points to him. There's nothing cuter than a man and a dog. I can work with this. I open his page and read that he's six feet tall (nice—although I'm short in stature, I do like a tall man), a mortgage broker (not that exciting but steady work, I guess), and twenty-seven years old (age appropriate, old enough to be ready to settle down). Also, he likes the beach and spends his weekends training his new puppy, Victor. Well, that's adorable. Before stopping to think too much about it, I send him an instant message.

"Hi, you and your dog are cute!" Did I just write that? I blame the alcoholic iced tea. Beyond mortified that I sent that message to a complete stranger, I go to close my laptop in shame when I receive a reply.

"Hi! You're cute too." What? Well, this is exciting. Deciding to embrace the courage provided to me by two potent drinks, I message back.

"Thanks. Are you free for a drink later this week?" My alcohol-fuelled confidence is making me feel bold. Which is a foreign but not an entirely unwelcome feeling for me.

"Sure, let's set something up," comes his reply. Wow! That was easy.

After a few messages back and forth, I find out that the cute Man with Dog is named Grant and that he lives nearby. He likes to try new restaurants, so he suggests we meet on Friday at a funky new bar and grill in the city, only a fifteen-minute drive from where I live. Happy with the way this is going, because I, too, love trying new places to eat, I agree, and we decide to confirm with each other later in the week.

I now feel very pleased with myself, knowing I'm on my way to crossing items one, two, and four off my to-do list, and as I close my computer and drain the rest of my drink, I decide to head to bed. I don't want to risk falling asleep on the couch for the second night in a row. As I make myself comfortable in bed, I grab my phone and check the Instagram notifications that appear to have been flooding in for my newly formed Love, Lilly page, and they seem to be coming in via the Market Place tag. Look at me, I'm a marketing genius! As I log in, I'm shocked to see the account already has over one thousand followers and that the first post is filled with comments. A lot are about the cookies, with some people boasting how they taste as good as they look (I have fans!) and some commenting on how cute I look (this photo is working for me tonight), and then there it is, among the drool face emojis and the "you're hot" comments—one that catches my attention:

It's from Oliver, and it says, "It is impossible to not Love Lilly :)"

Oh, Oliver, what are you doing to me? Here I am, making such good progress, and now, with that one comment, crossing number four off my list feels like an impossible task.

CHAPTER 12

Oliver

A s I sit on my bed, staring at my Instagram news feed, which is open on my phone, I look at the photo Lilly has just posted on the Love, Lilly page she created. The photo I took of her. She's so damn beautiful, with her big smile, the one that causes her nose to crinkle just a little. With her hair in a braid and her sun-kissed skin, she radiates happiness, and it's not surprising that the post has racked up over one thousand likes and comments already. Many of them from admiring men, I note.

I look at the comment I just wrote under her post and feel nauseous. What possessed me to write something as provocative as that? And even as I stress about this, I can't find it in me to delete it. It's true: in my mind, it's impossible to not love Lilly. It's just so unlike me to declare it to the World Wide Web. But this is what being around Lilly too much does to me. She makes me lose my mind! It's one of the reasons I decided way back when to not pursue a relationship with her. I knew instinctively that being with her would mean losing a big part of me, and I've never been brave enough to take that step.

This is in addition to the fact that even if I were brave enough to try to move us out of the friend zone, I've never been certain Lilly would even give me a chance. I've seen the guys she's dated in the past. They are all the opposite of me. Sporty, adventurous types. The kinds of guys who would whisk her away for a romantic weekend at the drop of a hat. Whereas I'd need at least a month of planning to allow that to happen. Why would spontaneous, fun-loving Lilly ever say yes to a date with someone as ordinary as me?

I hear a knock and look up to see Amy poking her head around the door. "Hey, Ol. You still up?"

I put my phone face down on the bed to hide what I was looking at and beckon Amy in. "What's up?"

Amy walks over and flops down on the bed next to me. "I just wanted to thank you for all the help you've given Lilly with her business. You've gone above and beyond for her this past week, what with the logo and everything."

With Amy giving me a smug smile, I shift, uncomfortable with where this conversation may be heading.

"That's what friends are for."

Amy continues to give me a smug look and goes to say something else, no doubt in reference to my feelings being more than friendly. Amy has always suspected that my feelings for Lilly run deeper than just friendly but has never come right out and challenged me about them. Given that I want to keep it that way, I cut her off before she can get started, not in the mood to be poked and prodded tonight.

"So are you going to call the lemonade guy?"

Amy groans and buries her head in one of my pillows. "I don't think so."

"Why? Even as a guy, I can say that dude was good looking," I tell her, chuckling at the look on her face.

"Hmmm," Amy replies, not maintaining eye contact with me. "Not interested."

"Could it be you are interested in someone else? Someone closer to home, or work?" I ask, turning the tables on her. It's clear as day that Amy has a mega-sized crush on her colleague and is just too stubborn to admit it.

Amy narrows her eyes at me, and I tense, knowing I've woken the beast. "Nice comment on Lilly's Instagram page." Bullseye.

"I don't know what you mean," I tell her as innocently as possible while I groan internally. I knew that comment was going to cause trouble!

"Uh-huh, that's the story you're going with? OK, what about Dale? He's cute, and he seems interested in Lilly. Should we try to play matchmaker?"

I know I'd rather set my hair on fire than set Lilly up on a date, so having had enough of this conversation, I make a noncommittal sound and get up to open my door, gesturing Amy towards it.

"As much as I've enjoyed this little chat, it's time for me to get some sleep. Long day and all. Work tomorrow..."

Amy shakes her head at me and, dragging her feet, makes her way towards my door.

"You know, you can't wait forever," she says as her parting shot.

I continue to feign ignorance. "Goodnight, Ames."

With a sigh, she leaves me with my thoughts. My stupid, confused, all-over-the-place thoughts. I hate feeling this way! I know I can't wait forever if I want to make a move on Lilly, but I only just sort of broke up with Emma (though apparently the jury is still out on that decision, and I'm awaiting an email with further instructions regarding our relationship status), and even if I were to become single, there are so many things to consider with Lilly.

The first one being, what if I'm not enough for her? Lilly is so special. She deserves someone who matches her outgoing, friendly nature, and while I can acknowledge I'm a good guy most of the time, am I the right guy for someone as effervescent as her?

And second, what if we try and we don't work out? What would become of our friendship? I can't imagine a life without Lilly in it. Am I willing to take a chance and risk losing her altogether? These are all the things that have held me back from pursuing something with Lilly over the years.

And then to add to my emotional turmoil is the level of jealousy I felt today when Dale showed up at the Market Place. Dale and I have grown to be good friends since we both joined the company at the same time a few years ago. Several months ago, I made the mistake of telling him about my feelings for Lilly, after too many beers had loosened my tongue at an after-work drinks session. And since then, he has been on my case to do something about it. This intensified when I told him Emma and I are "on a break" Ross-and-Rachel style, and he has been pushing me to finally "grow a pair" and make a move on Lilly ever since. I guess today's little display was his attempt at nudging me in the right direction. And it worked. When I saw him flirt with Lilly and had to witness her response, it was a jolt to my system. And how's it even possible that someone as special as Lilly is still single? And how long until that changes? Pretty soon, the man flirting with Lilly won't be a good friend of mine but someone who has actual intentions of claiming Lilly as their own. My stomach churns at the thought of losing Lilly, although I know she deserves to be with someone who knows how special she is, someone who will treat her right. Is that someone me?

I pick up my phone again and look at the photo in my hand, lying back in bed with a groan. I think to myself, Seriously, what am I going to do about you, Lilly?

CHAPTER 13

Lilly

THE WORKING WEEK DRAGS, AND after the fun of the Love, Lilly market stall on Sunday, it feels painful to be stuck in an office all day making photocopies and getting coffee for buffoon bosses who can't stop leering at me with their X-ray eyes. I keep my mind occupied with expanding my Love, Lilly social media presence and have added a TikTok account to the mix. Though I don't fully understand TikTok, it's imperative that I figure it out, as it seems to be the place all the cool kids hang out.

After the first Market Place tagged Instagram post, I found out that a semi-famous Instagram influencer with half a million followers visited my stall on Sunday. And she loved the brownies and raved about them in a post, tagging my account in the process. Since then, Love, Lilly has blown up. Literally. By Monday night, I had ten thousand followers, and now I feel the pressure to deliver some good content to make sure I don't lose them. To continue to capture the attention of my new audience, I decided to try a quick live baking tutorial video, as Oliver suggested, and that was liked by almost five thousand people, urging me to do them more regularly. I can work with this. It would seem that I enjoy being on camera when it involves doing something I love.

I've also been dedicating my lunch breaks to researching pop-up café options in the local area and am excited to have found that if I budget and save a good portion of my salary, I should have enough money to reserve a pop-up spot every month, opening in just a couple of months from now. And then there are the thoughts of my upcoming Friday night date to deal with. Since waking up with a Long Island Iced Tea hangover on Monday morning—must remember not to drink on a school night—and the memory of making a date, I've swung back and forth between excitement and dread. I know I need to get out there and meet people if I have any chance of moving on from my Oliver crush, but at the same time, an almost blind date with a stranger from the Internet isn't appealing.

"Miss Hamilton?" Mr Toad Face butts into my thoughts with what is, without a doubt, another ridiculous request for me to do something mundane for him. "Can you please staple these documents together and bring them to my office?" See?

I curse this useless frog man in my head, taking the papers from him, and in a sickly-sweet voice, I reply, "Of course, Mr Franklin. I'll do that right away." I watch as he saunters back to his office, muttering obscenities under my breath, feeling more certain than ever that I have to get out of here. Grabbing the stapler with annoyance, I look at my phone as I get a text message from Amy.

AMY: So have you thought about what you're going to wear on Friday night?

With only three days before my impending date, I have no time to go out and buy a date-appropriate outfit and have been, in my mind, browsing through my wardrobe, hoping there's something cute and sexy in there that I can pull together.

LILLY: No! Not yet. Thoughts?

AMY: I'm looping in the gang.

THERE'S a pause before the next text.

MADI: Wear something short, to show off your legs!

AMY: And something that showcases your boobs! Oh, and your tiny waist!

Sammi sends a fire emoji.

From this description, it sounds like I won't be wearing very much.

AMY: We'll help you put together the perfect outfit.

Amy is very excited about my getting back out there. She squealed like a little piglet when I told her about it.

AMY: Want to borrow something of mine? Or we can go shopping? Please let me take you shopping!

MADI: Girls' shopping trip?!

SAMMI: I'm in!

Unlike me, my friends love shopping and dressing up, while I'm happy to be in anything comfortable. And, as I have been advised by my know-it-all friends, diving back into the dating pool means dressing for comfort must now take a back seat.

LILLY: No time and no money for shopping. And, Ames, your clothes are always too tight around my bust and too long on my little legs.

AMY: The bust thing does not sound like an issue to me;).

SAMMI: :)

LILLY: I think I'll take it from here. Thanks, guys.

AMY: Send us pictures of your options and we can all decide.

MADI: Yes, loop us all in. We can take a vote. Majority rules.

LILLY: OK, will do. Got to go, boss man needs me to staple something for him :(.

AMY: You need a new job!

Sammi sends a GIF of a sad-looking puppy nodding.

LILLY: I'm working on it.

I sigh and put down my phone, getting back to the very important task of stapling documents. I love my life.

Later that night, I stand in front of my wardrobe and sort through my options. Hmm, each one is too tight or too short or too comfortable. What was I thinking when I purchased half these things? This is going to be harder than I thought. Just when I think all is hopeless, I spy a red miniskirt in the back of my cupboard. Madi told me a miniskirt is the way to go. The skirt is a perfect shade of red, not too bright but just bold enough to make a statement. I pair it with an off-the-shoulder black top, both tight across the bust and loose enough to breathe in, and some sky-high heels I'll need to practice wearing before Friday. The heels feel necessary given that Grant has said he's over six feet tall and I need to not feel like a hobbit next to him. Once I have it all on together, I take a picture of me wearing the outfit and send it to the girls for their approval.

With that settled, feeling a bit more confident about my clothing plans, I focus instead on Love, Lilly and how to capitalise on the fact that the brand has become Insta famous (it's a thing!). In the last few days, I have been getting flooded with messages, comments, and DMs from people wanting to know how they can get their hands on my treats. With this amount of engagement, I'm trying to turn my popularity into a way to make money. I know I need the help of someone who is an expert in marketing, and my mind goes straight to Oliver, though if I'm honest, my mind doesn't often stray away from him these days. I send him a quick text asking him the best way to make money from being Instagram famous. In typical Oliver fashion, he replies it isn't something he can detail over text, so we lock in a lunch date tomorrow to discuss potential strategies. With this in place, I sigh to myself, knowing that all this time I'm spending with Oliver isn't helping me check off number four on my to-do list but also understanding this is a necessary step to get numbers one and two done. What a conundrum I've made for myself.

With this step sorted, I continue to scroll through my most recent posts, and I stop on a picture I posted of me, Amy, and Oliver at my Love, Lilly stall, all smiling, surrounded by sugary goodness. Oliver has his arm around me, and I'm resting my head on his chest, beaming so much it almost hurts to look at me. This post generated quite a lot of attention, with many people wanting to know who the "hottie" in the photo is and how long we've been together. I haven't tagged Oliver in the post, so I'm hoping he hasn't seen these messages, knowing that Emma wouldn't be pleased. So far, he hasn't asked me to take it down, so I'm assuming he hasn't seen it yet. After looking at the photo again, I can say we make such a great-looking couple. I gratefully get distracted when the girls message me back with thoughts on my date night attire, filled with make-up and hair suggestions. I sigh and pick up the phone to do a group call, knowing they won't leave me alone until they have an approved head-to-toe look ready for me to go on Friday.

Now that I have a plan to meet Oliver for lunch, my painful morning moves at a snail's pace. Each minute feels like an hour, each hour like a day, and so on, until finally I can put the out-of-office message on my phone for the sixty minutes I get allocated for lunch and skip out of there. Oliver is sitting and waiting for me at a local café, and I have to stop myself short to catch my breath. Both from the skipping and from the sight of him. He's in what I'd term business casual, a white dress shirt, sleeves rolled up to mid-forearm—who knew forearms could be so sexy?—and a pair of grey pants. Simple, but on Oliver, it all looks delicious.

I approach him with caution, attempting not to throw myself at him, and go to sit down across from him, trying to act like a normal human being. As it happens, it would seem that I'm not one of those, and in the process of Oliver leaning over to kiss me hello and my attempting to sit down—which let's face it, shouldn't be so hard—I headbutt Oliver and end up missing the chair, landing on the floor. Hard.

"Lilly!" Oliver looks down at me with concern, rubbing the spot on his head where I headbutted him. "Are you OK?"

Why am I this way? I think as I pick myself up from the floor, cheeks and tail bone burning. Everyone is staring at us, and I sink into my seat, head in my hands.

"Lilly?" Oliver says in a soft voice. "Are you hurt?"

I shake my head, still unable to look up at him, and whisper, "Any chance you didn't see that?"

Oliver snorts with laughter, trying to cover the sound with a cough.

"See what?" he asks, playing along.

I allow myself a tiny, rueful smile, looking at him and saying, "Oh, nothing much. Just another impressive display of my co-ordination."

"You're a very graceful faller."

"Why thank you, I've had years of practice," I tell him, my mortification fading as we banter back and forth.

"Are you sure you are OK?" Oliver asks one more time, concern still written on his face.

Even though I'm almost certain my tail bone is broken and I may never sit without pain again, I give him a dismissive nod.

"Yes, yes, fine. Let's just order, shall we?"

I distract myself with the menu, talking through what I want to eat under my breath. "Focaccia or a sandwich? Focaccia or a sandwich?"

I glance up and see Oliver watching me with a soft look in his eyes. "Want to get both?"

I give him a wide smile and an eager nod. I hate having to choose between two good options; both is always best.

Once we have ordered, I broach the subject of Dale, to get a sense of how Oliver feels about our interaction at the Market Place.

"So your friend Dale seems nice."

Oliver's cheeks flush a bit as his gaze darts around the room, refusing to make contact with mine. "Does he?"

At his reply, I let out a small laugh. "Well, he's your friend. Shouldn't you think he's nice?"

At this, his big brown eyes snap to mine, and he pays me close attention. "Why the sudden interest? Would you like to get to know him better?"

Now with the tables turned on me, I backtrack out of this conversation by taking the food that has just arrived.

"Never mind, just making conversation," I tell him around a mouthful of toasted sandwich goodness.

Oliver also takes his food and the path out of this awkwardness, and while we eat our shared lunch, he outlines the best strategies for profiting from Instagram and general social media popularity.

"You need to get sponsorship deals, where you either get paid to post an advertisement, which is ideal. That is a pay-per-ad deal. Or you could post particular items as an influencer ad and offer a discount code. Any time one of your followers uses that code to purchase said item, you get a percentage of that purchase."

I look at Oliver as he pulls out a detailed synopsis of all the research he has done on this, and I think to myself, not for the first or hundredth time, that Emma is the luckiest woman alive.

"Thank you, Ollie," I tell him when he's done with his presentation, forever grateful for the amount of effort he has put towards this. "This has cleared up so much for me. I've already had a few companies reach out to me for these sorts of sponsorships. I thought they were a scam; you know, like the Nigerian prince asking for money?" Oliver laughs at this, his dimples flashing, like little beacons of happiness. "So I ignored them. I'll go back now and have a proper look."

"You can send me through any offers and I can have a look through them." Ever Mr Helpful.

As my lunch hour comes to an end, knowing the reaction I'll get from Mr Toad Face if I'm one minute late, I thank Oliver again and get to my feet, feeling my tail bone throbbing. Is a tail bone actually a bone that can break? I think to myself with some concern. I try to limp in as subtle a way as possible as I say goodbye to Oliver, feeling all warm and chocolaty gooey inside at the lengths he seems to be willing to go to make this a success for me. With each painful step I make towards the office, I'm now more confident that I won't have to work there for much longer.

CHAPTER 14

THE NEXT DAY, AFTER ANOTHER eternity of eight hours at the office, I attempt to distract myself from any thoughts of both Oliver and the trepidation surrounding my upcoming date and decide to visit Amy at the hospital and take her some cake to brighten up her evening. I choose to bake her a carrot cake because, you know, it's a hospital and carrots are healthy. I send a text to Amy to find out when she'll have time for a break and make my way to the emergency room for an emergency catchup.

When I get there, I'm struck, as I always am, by how frantic the place looks. Everyone is moving at pace, yet it all comes together like a well-choreographed dance. Amy's face lights up when she spots me and the cake in my hand and motions me to the break room.

"I'll be there in a few minutes," she calls out.

As I settle in one of the hard plastic chairs in the break room—they don't look like this on Grey's Anatomy—I scroll through my phone while I wait for her, hoping that maybe Grant has contacted me to cancel our upcoming date. It's not a good sign that I want the date to be over before it's even begun.

"Sorry about that, busy night tonight," Amy says, out of breath, as she takes a seat across from me, reaching for the cake with eager hands.

"It's carrot cake," I tell her, sliding it across the table. "Vegetables are good for you," I add with a smile.

Amy laughs as she takes a bite and groans. "Yes, the lemon cream cheese frosting tastes utterly healthy."

Before she has finished her second bite, I rush to ask her, "Can a person break their tail bone?"

Amy pauses in the act of swallowing a huge mouthful of cake and gives me a smile that suggests she knows exactly why I'm asking.

"Had a bit of trouble sitting in a chair recently?" she asks with a laugh.

"Shut up! It hurts," I tell her, attempting discreetly to rub the bruise that has developed overnight.

"You should be fine. Let me know if it gets any worse." She leans back with a sigh and rubs her tired eyes.

"Busy night?" I ask.

Amy nods. "It's always busy here, but tonight has been manic. I think it must be a full moon or something. We're filled to the brim with lots of crazy cases."

I lean forward, ready to hear all about it, and motion for her to tell me more.

"Well, the evening started off with a bang, literally, when a teenager came in having let off fireworks in his hands." I wince and laugh at the same time. "And then there's the guy who was high on something and thought he could fly, so he jumped off his roof, wearing only a cape no less, and broke his leg. And then there were the thirteen geniuses from a local university party who came in with 'food poisoning.' Turns out, from what they were throwing up, they poisoned themselves with a lot of Jell-O shots and vodka."

I laugh at her description and once again marvel at what Amy does on a daily basis.

"You're amazing, Amy," I tell her, filled with quiet awe.

"Who's amazing?" comes a deep masculine voice from behind us. "Are you talking about our Amy here?"

Amy stiffens in her seat, and I turn to see Dr McHottie make his way over to us.

"Don't give her too many compliments. Her head is big enough already," he finishes, patting her on the head and subtly stroking her hair, but he removes his hand when he sees me watching. Amy jerks her head away from him and mutters under her breath.

"And who do we have here?" Dr McHottie turns his attention to me, and I finally get a good look at him. Holy hotness, this guy is gorgeous. Like otherworldly gorgeous. No wonder he's causing Amy so much angst. I look up at his six-foot-plus frame and stare into his dark-blue eyes, taking in his high cheekbones, his chiselled jawline, and his salt-and-pepper hair. This guy is McDreamy and McSteamy combined.

"You must be Lilly. I'm Lucas. I work with Amy," he says with a slight accent (Italian?), reaching out to shake my hand with a genuine smile. Is that a gap between his front teeth? Oh no, Amy is a sucker for a front tooth gap.

Tongue-tied by what's in front of me, I nod dumbly.

"Hi!" I squeak at last.

Across from me, Amy rolls her eyes and sighs at me.

"Yes, this is Lilly." She draws out her words. Like it pains her to share any part of her life with him.

"It's a pleasure to meet you. I've heard a lot of great things about you. Not from Amy here herself," he tells me, nodding in her direction, "but from what I hear her tell other people."

I squeeze out an uneasy smile, looking between the two of them, noticing the palpable chemistry in the air.

"Well, it's nice to meet you too," I say, anything to break the tension in the room.

As Lucas is about to say something more, his beeper goes off. He frowns as he looks down at it and says to me, "Sorry, Lilly. I would have liked to stay and chat, but I have to go." At this, he turns and rushes out of the room, taking all his ridiculous hotness with him.

After he leaves, I stare at Amy, who isn't looking at me, and finally say, "Amy, that man is—"

"I know," she says, her voice dripping with misery.

"Do you want to talk about it?"

"Nope! Do you want to talk about—"

"Nope!"

"OK, so we won't talk about it. We're good. Everything is good."

"Yes," I agree after some hesitation. "Everything is great."

"Maybe I will call lemonade guy after all," Amy declares out of nowhere.

"Good, yes, you should. And I'm most definitely looking forward to my date with Grant tomorrow."

We look at each other with forlorn expressions plastered on our faces, then proceed to finish the entire cake in silence.

Friday finally arrives, now about as welcome as rain at a picnic, and the day wears on, bringing me closer to blind date central. I attempt to calm my nerves with meditation podcasts and deep breathing. I'm not sure why I'm so anxious about this date; it could be because the last time I dated, it ended in heartbreak and despair, or it could be because I know I'm entering this situation for the wrong reasons. I, while under the influence of a dodgy home-mixed cocktail, decided to start dating again with the sole motivation of getting over someone, not focusing on what would happen once I was actually "out there." Ugh, I need to get out of my head and just enjoy this time and what it could mean. And, worst-case scenario, I may get a free meal at a restaurant that I've been dying to go to for weeks.

At home, among a cloud of clothes and hairspray, with the girls sending me encouraging text messages and inappropriate memes, I get a text message from Oliver. My heart skips a little beat as I open it.

OLIVER: Big date tonight, I hear?

LILLY: Amy has a big mouth :)

OLIVER: So who's the lucky guy?

LILLY: No one you know, no one I know. Just someone I met online.

A moment later, Oliver's face appears on my screen as I answer his FaceTime call.

"You're going on a blind date?" Oliver asks.

"Well, that's generally what happens when you connect online. It's essentially blind. Though, I have seen his picture, and he seems nice," I reply, distracted as I attempt to coax my hair into some semblance of order. Amy said beach waves are on trend now, so maybe I should just leave my hair alone? Because that's all I can seem to get it to do tonight.

"But you don't know him? What if he's a serial killer?" Oliver asks, pulling me back into the conversation. Huh, I hadn't even thought of that.

"He doesn't look like a serial killer," I say. "He looks pretty cute. I'm sure I'll be fine."

"That's probably what Ted Bundy's victims thought too. Maybe you should cancel."

I stop fiddling with my hair to focus in on what Oliver is saying, picking up that he looks worried for me, among another emotion, one I can't place.

"I'll be fine, Ollie. We're meeting in a popular restaurant, with lots of people around. I'll watch my drinks around him and leave if I get any crazy stalker vibes from him. OK?" I add when he remains looking unconvinced.

"Are you sure you want to do this?" he asks. "You've never been interested in this online dating stuff before."

"It's time for me to get back out there and meet people. I'm never going to meet 'the one' hanging out with you and Amy. Not that being with you guys isn't fun," I add when he winces. "I just need to find someone for me."

Oliver looks like he's going to argue and stops himself. He pauses and just looks at me for a long moment before saying in a soft voice, "You look beautiful tonight, Lilly." My breath catches at his compliment, and I stare at him in silence for a beat. When it looks like we have nothing else to say to each other, and now that he has messed with my mind just before my date, Oliver says goodbye.

"Be careful tonight, Lilly. And don't forget to make sure your phone is fully charged, just in case you need rescuing." And with that, he disconnects the phone. I blow out a deep breath and get back to the task of getting ready, my heart no longer in this date at all.

CHAPTER 15

Lilly

T WO HOURS AND TWO GLASSES of wine later, I'm waiting at the bar of this very nice restaurant, tapping the toe of my stiletto heel impatiently against the leg of the bar stool. Grant is late. And not just "stuck in traffic" late, but "I'm too important to be on time" late. At first, I thought maybe he was trying to find a car park, something I did not have to worry about, having decided against driving to the restaurant and to take an Uber instead, and I cut him some slack, but that was twenty minutes ago. When does being late turn into being stood up? And I can't even pretend to look busy by scrolling on my phone, as it is at this very moment sitting at home plugged into the charger. Thank you for that, Oliver. Deciding to just call it a night, I glance down at the menu in order to get some takeaway food to bring home with me, with plans to spend the rest of the evening on the couch looking up nearby convents to join, when I hear my name. I look up and see someone who vaguely resembles Grant making his way across to the restaurant to where I'm sitting. Maybe Grant's shorter, older, less good-looking cousin is here to meet me and tell me Grant has been in a terrible accident, or something similar, and couldn't make our date?

"Lilly, is that you?" Pseudo-Grant asks when he stops in front of me.

"Uh, yes?" I reply, my voice filled with suspicion. Who is this guy?

"Wow, you look just like your photo. That almost never happens," he replies with a happy grin. Wait, is this guy actually Grant?

No way this guy is Grant!

"Grant?" I ask, filled with disbelief. This guy looks nothing like the guy in the puppy photo. That guy had muscles apparent from his tight T-shirt. And he had hair. The guy in front of me is sporting an impressive beer gut and is definitely trying to cover up a receding hairline with a rough-looking comb over. Ugh. This is the worst.

"Yes, it's me." He grins, looking me up and down like he just won the lottery. "Have you been waiting long? I was just sitting outside on the phone when I noticed the time."

Great, this guy isn't just misrepresenting himself to hapless women online, but he's arrogant to boot.

"I'm really sorry for keeping you waiting," he adds, perhaps noticing my unimpressed expression. "I hope I haven't blown this." He nervously pats his thinning hair.

With a feeling of remorse, both for judging him on his tardiness (I'm usually the late one, so I guess I can cut him some more slack), and for being so superficial about his looks, I decide to start the night fresh. So I hop off my stool and say, "That's OK, do you want to grab a table and get something to eat?"

Grant 2.0, as I now refer to him in my mind, releases a relieved breath and smiles. "That sounds great. Shall we?" He waves me past him, and as I walk by, I note he's not much taller than me in my heels. Which makes him five feet seven at the most. Six feet tall, my arse.

To get the date back on track, I make small talk with Grant 2.0 while we look at the menu. Given I already read it front to back twenty times in the last hour and pretty much have it committed to memory now, I watch with increasing impatience as Grant deliberates what he wants to eat. The waitress gives a loud sigh as she waits to take his order, and I feel like kicking him under the table to make him get a move on. I'm at the point of being hangry.

"I'll have the steak, well done. And a side of fries. No salad," he orders finally, having spent five long, agonising minutes to settle on the most boring food option on the menu. I decide to be more adventurous and order the seafood risotto with a side of garlic-roasted Brussels sprouts.

"I like a girl that can eat," Grant 2.0 declares after our waitress leaves, sparing me a sympathetic glance as she goes. This terrible date must be obvious for everyone to see. "I hate those stick-skinny girls who only eat lettuce," he adds with unfounded bravado, looking at me like he wants recognition for being so evolved.

"I think a man or woman should eat what they want," I reply, "even if that's just lettuce. Who are we to judge?" I add, giving him a pointed look.

"Right, right," he backtracks. "Very true."

We sit in silence for a moment, me because I'm uncomfortable and Grant 2.0 because he's on his phone. Is this guy serious?

"So, Grant," I say in a loud voice, causing him to jump and pulling his attention off his screen. "Tell me a bit more about what you do for work." Big mistake, Lilly. For the next twenty minutes, I'm forced to listen to Grant drone on and on about mortgages and interest rates and the Reserve Bank and... Oh, look, here's our food. I hope that having something in his mouth might shut Grant up for a bit as I dig into my risotto, groaning in delight. This dish almost makes this whole horrible night worth it.

"You like that, hey?" Grant 2.0 says with a suggestive wink. Oh, gross.

"Yes, it's delicious," I reply, not engaging with his innuendo. "How's your steak?"

Grant 2.0 uses this opportunity to tell me all about his knowledge of beef and the best way to grill a steak, and hey, do you want to learn all about my new barbecue and its smoking feature? I sigh, bored out of my mind, wondering how long I have to sit here until I can leave. Basic politeness dictates that I finish my meal, even though I don't owe this guy anything. As I tune back in, I hear that Grant 2.0 has moved on to another apparent favourite topic of his, sports. Oh boy, this is going to be a long night.

When Grant 2.0 finally finishes his meal, taking extra long to get through it because he has spent so much time recounting the play-by-play of the latest football- / basketball- / something-ball that happened last night, I decide it's time to go. This date is done.

"Would you like to come back to my place for a coffee or dessert? Maybe Netflix and chill?" he asks, clueless to the situation at hand, and also, who uses the phrase "Netflix and chill" on a date?

"No thanks, Grant. Early start tomorrow and all." I lean down to reach for my bag as a hint that this night is over. O-V-E-R, over.

"Oh, you're one of those girls." His face takes on a mean expression. "You flirt with a guy online, and then when the time comes for some action, you play hard to get."

Is this guy for real?

"No, Grant, that's not the situation here. You appear to be functioning under a false impression of what meeting up for a date is all about," I tell him, my voice rising along with my temper. "We had dinner, some not-so-interesting conversation," I add, spearing him with a look. "And now it's time to part ways."

"Fine," he says with an attitude. "I'm just going to the bathroom, and then we can leave." And he gets up and walks away from the table. As my gaze follows him, I watch in complete shock as he walks in the opposite direction of the bathroom and straight out the front door. Did he seriously just walk out and leave me to pay the whole bill? What is happening right now?

I rub my temples, trying to stem the beginnings of a headache forming there, and decide on the spot to take an indefinite hiatus from dating. As I reach down for my purse to pay the bill, my hand encounters only air where my bag should be. Hang on! Where's my bag? In a swift motion, I look under and around the table, but it's not there where I left it. I grab the waitress as she walks by and ask her with quiet desperation in my voice, "Has anyone turned in a handbag? It was a cute black leather bag with a red zip?"

She gives me a sad shake of her head when she sees that my loser date has gone.

"This is some dreadful night you're having, hey hon?" she says with sympathy, popping the gum in her mouth.

I take a minute to gather my thoughts, absorbing the fact that I now have no money to pay for the meal or an Uber, no phone to call a friend for help, and therefore no way of getting home, and say to the waitress, "You've got that right. Can I use your phone?"

Without my mobile phone and its comprehensive list of contacts, I call the only number I know from memory (other than my parents'). Please pick up, Amy. "You have reached Amy and Oliver.

We're not here at the moment. Please leave a message, and we will get back to you." Damn it.

"Uh. Hi, Amy, are you there? It's Lilly. Now isn't the time to be screening your landline calls. I'm not a telemarketer..." I pause, hoping she will pick up. "OK, you obviously aren't home," I say after a beat. "I've gotten myself into a little bit of a sticky situation, and I kind of need your help. This date was really bad, by the way. Anyway, I'm a bit stuck—"

"Lilly? Is that you? Are you OK?" Oliver's voice comes on the line, filled with urgency.

"Yes, Ollie, it's me," I reply with resignation, knowing I'm going to need to ask him for help. Again.

"Where are you? Why are you calling on the landline? What happened to your date? Are you OK?" he fires off.

"Oliver," I interrupt his rapid-fire questions. "I'm fine. I'm sorry to call you on your Friday night. It's just that my loser date left unexpectedly, leaving me with the bill no less, and I may have been mugged." Is it called mugging if your bag just disappears? I wonder to myself. "And I don't have my mobile phone because someone told me I needed to charge it before I left, and that's where it now remains, at home on the bench." I trail off. "Oliver? Are you still there?"

There's another moment of silence as Oliver obviously collects himself.

"So you're telling me that you're stranded, with no phone or money, after being mugged? After your date just left you there?"

"Well, you make it sound so dramatic. But really, I'm fine. Just a bit stuck." I look around, and the staff is starting to pack up for the night. "And I have no way to pay for the meals and no way to get home," I finish in a small voice.

"Lilly, tell me where you are, and I'll come and get you."

I tell him the name of the restaurant. "Thanks, Ollie, and sorry for the trouble I've caused."

More silence on Oliver's end before he adds, "Just stay there until I can get to you." And he hangs up. And I wait to be rescued again.

CHAPTER 16

Lilly

Fifteen minutes later, as I'm sitting chatting to my new friends who are busy cleaning up behind the bar, a harried-looking Oliver rushes into the restaurant and makes a beeline for me. He grabs me off the bar stool, looking me up and down with concern, before pulling me in for a full-body hug.

"Lilly, you had me worried," he says into my ear, pulling back only a small amount to look me in the eye. "Are you really OK?"

"Oh, sure, I'm fine. A bit embarrassed to be in this situation, but as my new friend Sally tells me," I say, pointing to the bartender behind the bar, "men suck."

Sally gives me an emphatic nod while she continues to clean the glasses. "They sure do, honey."

I turn to see that Oliver is still looking me up and down, focusing mostly on my legs in my high heels, almost mesmerised.

"I can walk in them," I tell him, hoping to put his mind at ease. "It's fine."

Oliver clears his throat and steps back from me. "Who do I need to pay so we can get you out of here?"

I point to Gabriel, another new friend, working behind the cash register, and say, "Thank you, Oliver. I'll pay you back." Oliver waves me away and goes to settle up my bill.

"He's a keeper, honey," Sally whispers to me from the bar.

I sigh as I follow her gaze. "Tell me something I don't know."

Once he has paid for both my and Grant 2.0's meals, Oliver takes my hand and guides me out of the restaurant, with me waving goodbye to my new friends and promising to come back and visit them. I settle into the front seat of Oliver's car, leaning my head back and closing my eyes. This night has been a complete disaster.

"Lil? Are you sure you're OK? Tell me what happened." As I fill Oliver in on the events of the night, including Grant walking out without saying goodbye, Oliver's hand tightens on his steering wheel.

"Lilly, you shouldn't be going out with guys like that," he tells me like it's something I don't know.

"I know that, Ol, but how will I know what a guy is going to be like until I meet him? This one seemed perfectly nice online. There were no indications that he was going to turn out to be a boring, bill-hopping possible kleptomaniac," I end with a small smile.

Oliver doesn't look amused. "You deserve so much better, Lil. You deserve to be with someone who will treat you right. Someone who's actually worthy of you."

I stare at Oliver, knowing he doesn't see that he's describing himself. "I'm aware that I deserve better. And maybe someday I will get that," I add in a soft, hope-filled voice. I turn my head away from Oliver to look out of the window, exhausted all of a sudden by everything that has just transpired, and notice the direction we are heading.

"Hey, where are we going?"

"I'm taking you back to our house. I assume your house key was in your bag and you won't be able to get into your apartment? And you shouldn't be alone in that neighbourhood," he adds under his breath, "after what you've been through tonight." Not having the energy or the will to fight him, I give a small nod and settle in for the car ride home.

When we arrive at the Harlow house, I hoist myself out of the car, and teetering on my ridiculous shoes, I walk up the driveway, with Oliver holding my arm to steady me on the uneven surface.

"Amy will be home soon," Oliver tells me as he opens the front door.

"Great," I reply. "I think I need some girl talk."

Oliver watches me from over his shoulder as we walk into the front door, while my sole focus now is to get out of this outfit and forget all about this terrible night.

"That took long enough," a sharp voice cuts through the silence. Great. I look up to see Emma staring at me with disdain and shrink back against the wall.

"My fault, again," I say with a little wave, feeling stupid. "Just a date gone wrong," I add, hoping to garner her sympathy.

Emma gives me one final look of contempt and then ignores me, looking at Oliver with impatience.

"What took you so long? I've been here just waiting for you. We were supposed to spend the evening talking."

I look at Oliver's disgruntled expression and realise he left his evening with Emma to come and get me and, in my mind, let out a miserable groan.

"Once again," I call out, my voice coming out louder than expected, "it was my fault. I kind of got mugged—well, sort of mugged, really, maybe just pickpocketed?" I ramble on. "And I didn't have my phone or any money, so I called here looking for Amy, and Ollie here picked up and came to help me," I finish, knowing that my tale of woe isn't going to go over well with this audience.

"Oliver makes quite the habit of 'helping' you, Lilly," she says—she got my name right!

"Are you completely incapable of looking after yourself?" she adds. Ouch, she's so mean.

Before I can answer, Oliver snaps, "That's enough, Emma! We'll talk about this later." He turns to look at me. "You've had a long night. Why don't you rest in Amy's room? She should be home any minute."

I smile again at Oliver and cast an uncertain, wary look back at Emma, heading up the stairs. "Sorry again for ruining your night, guys. It won't happen again." I say this with a confidence I don't feel, knowing I'll probably get myself into another situation that will require some sort of intervention again one day soon.

As I reach the top of the stairs and head for Amy's room, I hear the muffled sounds of angry voices as Oliver and Emma move into the kitchen and out of earshot. I hope I haven't gotten Oliver into too much trouble. I sit down on Amy's bed, taking off the torture shoes, and lie back with a sigh. What a night.

When I open my eyes a little while later, Amy is lying next to me, looking at me with concern. "Oliver filled me in on what happened tonight, Lil. Are you OK?" she asks in her gentle nurse voice when she sees I am awake.

"I'm fine," I say for what feels like the hundredth time tonight. "It's more mortifying than anything. Grant was such a loser; I should have left when he was almost an hour late."

"An hour?" Amy exclaims in horror. "That's terrible!"

"That's not the worst of it," I tell her, going on to share with her all the details, some of which I conveniently forgot to tell Oliver. "It was such a waste of time. And not only that, but I also managed to get Oliver into trouble with Emma." I fill her in on what happened when we got home.

"It sounds like they got into quite the argument after I left them," I finish.

"What's her problem, anyway?" Amy asks, a grumpy frown marring her face. "Why wouldn't she want her boyfriend to be kind and helpful?"

"I think she doesn't like that he is all those things to me," I reply before adding, trying to be fair, "and I can understand that. I've ruined quite a few of their dates in recent weeks."

"But you're his friend. He should be able to help you without risking his relationship," Amy says like a wise, old owl.

I agree with Amy, but not wanting to get into a debate about Oliver's relationship, I change the subject. "So now I have to sort out a locksmith to change the locks to my apartment. Luckily the only things I had thrown into my handbag before leaving were my house key, one hundred dollars, and my Starbucks loyalty card, so I don't have to worry about that part too much," I add, happy that I had left my full purse with all my credit cards and car keys at home in favour stuffing some cash in my small, impractical, but oh-so-cute handbag. Oh, cute handbag, I'll miss you.

"I'm glad you're here with us tonight," Amy says now. "You need a good night's sleep so you can rally and regroup tomorrow." She gets up and hands me an oversize T-shirt to sleep in as she gets into her own pyjamas.

"Thanks, Ames. You and your brother are my saviours," I say as I wiggle out of my date night clothes and slip the butter-soft T-shirt over my head. With a grateful sigh, I sink into Amy's bed and snuggle under the blanket. Closing my eyes, I finally let this day come to an end.

A few hours later, I wake up, disoriented and thirsty. Where am I? I look around and see that it's still dark and Amy is snoring next to me, and the events of my disastrous evening flash through my mind. I get up and head downstairs to get some water, and maybe a snack, stumbling around in the dim light, finally letting out a relieved sigh when I reach the kitchen without incident. I open the fridge door to shed some light around the space and stand on my tippy-toes to reach for the glasses on the top shelf, when muscular arms encircle me from behind.

"Need some help?" Oliver asks right into my ear.

"Oliver!" I hiss. "You scared me half to death." I turn to see his face close to mine, and he's wearing a wide smile.

"I can't reach the glasses," I announce. "This house is built for giant people." He grins at me even wider, shocking me further by picking me up and moving me to the side. Once he has safely deposited me back on the ground, he reaches up and grabs two glasses for us before filling them up in the sink.

"Couldn't sleep?" he asks, breaking the silence.

"Just thirsty, and maybe a bit hungry?" I take the glass of water from him. "Is there anything to eat in this fridge?" I ask with doubt, knowing there rarely is anything edible kept here, but I bend down to rummage through just in case.

"Ollie? Any snacks for me?" I ask again when he doesn't reply, turning to look at him. Oliver is standing where I left him, gazing at me, looking from the T-shirt to my bare legs and back again. Feeling acutely aware of my state of undress, knowing that I'm standing in front of him in only very small underwear and a T-shirt that keeps slipping off one shoulder, I turn back to the fridge, now looking for anything to break the tension.

"That's my T-shirt," Oliver finally says in a strangled voice.

I look at him, a blush spreading across my entire body. "Sorry, I didn't know. Amy gave it to me to wear." And then, in a lame attempt at a joke, I add, "Do you want it back?" I grab the bottom, acting like I'm going to lift it.

"No!" Oliver steps towards me, his hand reaching for his T-shirt. He slowly pulls the sleeve back up over my shoulder from where it slipped down, scorching my skin in the process. We both watch as he deliberately caresses my shoulder, almost mesmerised, the two of us illuminated by only the soft glow of the fridge light.

"It's yours now," he whispers in a hushed voice, still staring at where his hand just was.

After being struck dumb by what has just occurred, I finally find my voice and say, "I was just kidding, Ollie. I'll give it back. It's just for tonight."

"Don't worry about it," Oliver says, shaking his head and taking an abrupt step back from me, walking towards the kitchen door. "It looks better on you anyway," he adds as he gives me one last searching look and leaves the room. And I'm left feeling hot and bothered, aware that I'll never be able to get back to sleep now.

CHAPTER 17

Oliver

I LEAVE LILLY IN THE kitchen, wearing my clothes, and almost run to my bedroom. There's only so much temptation a man can take. Just seeing her there, all bare legs and tousled hair—she looked like a dream in my T-shirt. Oh, who am I kidding? Lilly looks like a dream to me wearing just about anything. And her skin is as soft as it looks. This is pure torture. I close and lock my door—ensuring I don't give in to every instinct urging me to go back out there, find Lilly, and kiss her senseless—and lie back on my bed with a sigh. It had been quite the evening.

It started with Lilly going out on a blind date. When Amy mentioned in passing that her friend was meeting up for dinner with some random guy, my stomach twisted with jealousy. This is just what Dale predicted would happen, that Lilly would meet someone else and I'd miss my opportunity. And this type of man, one eaten up with jealousy—well, it just isn't who I am. Or the way I know myself to be. I'm a calm and rational person, not someone who is prone to feelings of envy and fear. So, with this in mind, I spent most of the week trying to ignore my feelings, but after a few days of torture, where I just couldn't stop myself from picturing her out with another man, I caved and contacted her. I didn't have any plan in place for what I wanted to achieve with this phone call to Lilly, mere hours before her date, but I knew I had to stop her from going.

But then, seeing her all aglow with what appeared to be excitement about her upcoming date, I knew I had to rein it in a bit. Lilly, first and foremost, is my friend, and if she wants to go out with a stranger from the Internet, I have to trust her judgment to do so. So I talked myself out of talking her out of her date. And let her go out with that douche Grant, looking gorgeous in her miniskirt and slinky top. Seriously, Lilly in a miniskirt and heels is a sight to behold.

Distracted now, I get up and do some push-ups. Any way to get rid of the tension I've been feeling since I heard her voice on the answering machine. Lilly was out there stranded again, with no money and no phone. Still worked up, I flip onto my back and do some sit-ups as I picture her when I arrived to get her. I expected to find her crying and upset, but instead, she was sitting at the bar, chatting to the staff, laughing and telling jokes and making friends, like she hadn't been dealt a rubbish hand that night. And that's the thing about Lilly. She gets pushed down, but she never stays there. Her ability to always stay happy and positive is one of the things I love the most about her.

This did change, however, when we got home and Emma let her nasty side show again. And that was it. I was done. No more homework from Emma. The relationship was over. After sending Lilly upstairs and out of earshot, I told Emma in no uncertain terms that we were over. She yelled for a bit and cursed me out, and then she left in a huff. And finally, I was released from a relationship I probably shouldn't have been in in the first place.

Don't get me wrong, I do feel bad about what happened with Emma. And I tried to make it work with her over the course of our relationship, but when it comes down to it, I just can't help that it's Lilly I want to be with. And now that I've had that scare tonight with Lilly heading back out into the dating scene, and add that to seeing her in the kitchen just then, all rumpled in my T-shirt, it is solidified again in my mind that it's time to put aside all my concerns about being with Lilly and finally do something about making her mine.

CHAPTER 18

Lilly

THE NEXT MORNING, AFTER SPENDING the rest of the night tossing and turning, replaying the scene in the kitchen with Oliver repeatedly, I wake up feeling restless and annoyed. The entirety of last night was a bust. And now I have to deal with the consequences. I use Amy's phone to organise for a locksmith to meet me at my apartment, and after half dragging, half cajoling Amy out of bed to give me a lift home, I manage to get out of the house without another Oliver encounter. In my mind, it's now imperative that I avoid him for the foreseeable future, before this crush turns into something bigger.

Thirty minutes later, after thanking Amy for letting me crash in her bed and for driving me home, I greet the locksmith. With Johnny hovering in the background, making everyone nervous, the work gets done in record time, and then I'm back in my apartment with a new lock installed, ready to shower off the grime from the last twelve hours. Once clean and in my most comfortable yoga pants and sweatshirt, I send Oliver a message with an update on the lock situation, thanking him again for the rescue.

When he replies with a single thumbs-up emoji, I gather that Oliver, too, is needing some space. With extreme care, I put his T-shirt in the laundry basket, giving it one last stroke as I do—so soft—and then I grab my laptop to delete my profile from the dating website, feeling a sense of relief that I don't have to go through any of that again. If I can't meet someone out in the wild—what's so wrong with meeting someone at a bar anyway, like Meredith Grey and Derek Shepherd?—then I won't be meeting anyone at all. And right now, that seems more than fine to me.

Feeling somewhat dejected, I head to the kitchen to do what always soothes me when I'm feeling down, baking. Today I decide to take the time to make a special treat, one that involves a lot of concentration so my mind won't wander to places it's best not going. My baked vanilla cheesecake with raspberry coulis is always a big hit, so I set about measuring out ingredients, and to get rid of the deafening silence in my lonely apartment, I put on one of my favourite true crime podcasts, getting lost in the world of armchair detectives and unsolved murders.

Once the cheesecake is in the oven, the coulis is chilling in the fridge, and they've solved the case of the missing teenager, I look at the time and see that it's mid-afternoon, and I'm at a loss for how to fill the remaining hours. Is it too early to break open the wine? I'm messing around with my Love, Lilly Instagram page, working on my latest sponsorship ad for #bakeware, when I get a FaceTime call from my parents. I haven't spoken to them in weeks.

"Hi, Mum! Hi, Dad!" I say as both their faces fill my screen.

"Hello, Lilly," my mum replies.

"How are you? We were just saying that we haven't heard from you in a while," my dad adds.

Happy that they noticed I hadn't been in touch, I fill them in on the exciting progress I've been making with Love, Lilly.

"So I'm getting a lot of followers on Instagram and TikTok, which are already bringing in a small income through paid sponsorship ads. And this will all hopefully turn into a lot of customers in the future when I finally open up my own café," I finish up telling them. I look at my parents' faces and can see they're not sharing in my enthusiasm for my business venture, and though they don't say anything specifically negative about it, it becomes clear in their next line of questioning that this isn't something they support.

"Are you sure this is the career path you want to pursue? It's not exactly what you focused on when you went to university," my dad asks.

And what was that path? I ask my dad in my mind.

"It sounds risky, with no steady income or plans in place should it fail," my mum adds. They're an echo chamber of negativity.

I sigh to myself, resigned to the fact that they are already envisioning it will fail, and tell them, "I have a business plan in place, with all the financials worked out, projecting costs and revenue for the next six to twelve months, with contingency plans in place as well," I add, hoping to wow them with my foresight and business acumen. "I did major in business with two semesters of economics as part of my course, remember? This will help turn my small business idea into something real."

"Oh yes, the economics classes. I had forgotten you took those as part of your degree. Maybe there's a job out there where you can use that particular skill set?" my dad says, missing the point.

"She could go work as an intern in a financial institute, like the son of your colleague Darren. What's his son's name again?" Mum asks Dad, talking about me like I'm not there.

"Yes, Darren's son Brad. He started at the bottom and worked his way up," my dad clarifies. "That sounds like a wonderful idea for you, Lilly. You could really carve out a solid career for yourself in finance."

With a sad smile, I wonder how, knowing me, they could possibly see me working in finance, and I give them a noncommittal answer, wanting to end the conversation and get away from the stain of disappointment that always surrounds our conversations.

"I'd better go," I tell my parents as my oven timer goes off in the background, ever so grateful for a legitimate excuse to disconnect the phone call.

"I'll call you soon," I promise them.

"OK, bye, Lilly. Don't forget to investigate financial internships online. It's still early in the year, so you will have a chance to secure a spot. You need to do it now though. You don't want to miss out," my dad adds.

"Sure thing." I reply, forcing a smile. "Love you guys, bye!"

I hang up the phone and pull myself to my feet, feeling heavy with the weight of my parents' unfulfilled expectations. I take my beautifully crafted cheesecake out of the oven and place it on the bench. As I look at it, I'm filled with so much joy and pride, and I can't understand why my parents don't want me to feel this every day. I spend some time taking a photo of the result and post it to Instagram with the caption, "Expectations fulfilled." At least I'm good at something.

After I force myself to do some adulting, spending an hour folding laundry, vacuuming my entire apartment, and surface cleaning the bathroom, I allow myself to log back on to Instagram and scroll through my latest DMs. Most of them are asking for more videos and tutorials on baking made simple, so I pour myself a glass of wine—it's wine o'clock somewhere in the world—and, determined to give the people what they want, I look through my recipe cards. I settle on a favourite easy recipe of mine for "no-bake bliss balls" and pull together the ingredients, pressing the go-live button once I'm ready.

"Hello, friends," I say into the screen. "And welcome to my Love, Lilly lesson!"

As I watch the viewer numbers increasing to over one thousand and counting, I continue, "Today I'm going to walk you through the very easy three-step process to make bliss balls." I take another sip of wine, monitoring the comments as I begin guiding the audience through the recipe. I'm startled at how many people are commenting on how cute I look (in this outfit?), and my confidence grows. And once I've made my way through most of my glass of wine, my commentary predictably veers away from baking content, and soon I'm discussing my thoughts on what happened on the latest episode of The Bachelor.

"And can you believe Clayton broke up with both Gabby and Rachel? It just goes to show, give a guy thirty eligible women and he can still end up alone," I say, noticing that my viewership numbers have increased substantially throughout the video, with most of them loving the random, non-food-related commentary.

As I get to the last step, I wrap up by saying, "Once this is done, you just place them in an airtight container and put them in the fridge overnight." I smile at all the happy face emojis I'm seeing and finish up by saying, "I'll post this recipe on the Love, Lilly page, so keep an eye out for it. And please leave me a comment about what you'd like me to make next time. Or better yet, I may run a poll. Yes, that's what I'll do. So make sure you tune in next time for another dramatic episode of Love, Lilly Lessons," I finish up in my best Chris Harrison voice. I end the video to a wave of hearts and clapping hands emojis, and I feel excited and exhilarated in a way I haven't in the longest time.

That was amazing! I think to myself once I put down my phone and set about cleaning the kitchen. So many people logged on to view my Instagram Live, over fifteen thousand by the end, and now the comments and DMs are flooding in. With my third glass of wine in hand, feeling pretty good about myself, I settle onto the couch to read some messages from my adoring fans. As I glance down the list of usernames, my eyes and mind screech to a stop at one familiar one: Seb_Bedford_69. That can't be right, can it? Sebastian, my ex-boyfriend who stranded me in a cabin on a mountaintop and left me heartbroken all those months ago, messaging me on Instagram. When I look more closely, I see he has sent several DMs over the past week, with the last one from today saying,

Seb_Bedford_69: Hey Lilly, love seeing your face on the 'Gram.

I roll my eyes at how lame he sounds.

Seb_Bedford_69: Would be great to talk to you. I have something to tell you. Call me if you get this.

Well, this is an interesting twist. Given that I blocked his number after the sad trip down the mountain in Oliver's car, I have had no contact with him since then, and now he wants to talk? Does he want to get back together? Does he regret leaving me? The questions race through my mind as I drain the rest of my wine and consider my options. On the one hand, I don't want to talk to him, even if he were to beg to get me back. And on the other hand, I'm so curious that if I don't call now, I may just burst. I think about the best approach here, tempted to message the girls to get their guidance, and decide instead to just call him and find out what the hell he wants.

Filled with liquid courage, I call the number of the last guy who broke my heart and wait.

"Lilly? Is that you?" Sebastian answers on the third ring.

"Hi, Seb," I say, playing it cool.

"Lilly! It's so good to hear from you!" he says with enthusiasm. This is new. "Your Instagram posts and videos have been amazing!"

I feel a wave of pride wash over me at this compliment and respond with sincerity, "Thanks, Seb. So what's up?" I cut to the chase, not wanting to get stuck taking part in any small talk with him.

"Well," he starts. "I've been meaning to call you and have even sent you a few text messages, which you didn't reply to," he adds, almost accusingly.

"I had nothing to say to you," I respond. "And after the way we ended, I had nothing I wanted to hear from you either."

"Fair enough," he replies. "I just wanted to apologise for the way things ended. I know it was unexpected."

"You can say that again," I interject.

"Well, yes. You see, I wasn't forthcoming with you when we broke up that day, but the truth is that I had met someone else and I didn't want to cheat on you, so I thought it best to end it immediately."

"Do you want a medal for this?" I ask, my voice dripping with sarcasm. And then, thinking about what he said, I say, "Wait, you met someone else? Who?"

"She's someone I work with. She was just a friend, and then one day I looked at her and felt like I wanted to be more than friends. It wasn't any reflection on you, Lil. It's just that Sarah and

I have more in common, and with her, it's effortless. She's easy. She's amazing. I can't wait for you to meet her."

I feel the wind taken out of my sails as my insecurities come rushing back with a vengeance, and I can't find the words to reply. Meet her? Hell will freeze over before that happens.

"Lilly? Are you there? I haven't upset you, have I? Our breakup was so long ago," he says in a voice filled with false sympathy.

"Upset me?" I ask, rallying and wrapping my pride around me like a cloak. "Of course not. As you say, it was forever ago. We weren't that serious, and I moved on almost straightaway. Found the love of my life as well," I lie.

"That's great!" he says. "So it all worked out for both of us."

"I guess..."

"That brings me to my reason for getting in contact with you. You know I always thought of you as a good friend? Even before we got together." He did? I ask myself. "So I wanted to reach out and invite you to my wedding."

WEDDING? What is this man talking about?

"Your wedding?" I screech. Great way to play it cool, Lilly.

"Yes, Sarah and I are getting married in a couple of weeks, on Valentine's Day, and I'd love for you to be there."

"Wait, you and Sarah are engaged? But you can't be. You've only been together for like three minutes."

"When you meet the right person, you just know, you know?" he says with condescension.

"Oh yes," I say, backtracking. "Totally. That's how I feel about my boyfriend. We're so in love. I just know he's the one." Stop talking, Lilly.

"That's great to hear, Lil. You can bring your boyfriend with you. To the wedding. It's a full weekend event, and we'd love for you to be there."

Why? I think to myself. And also, there's no way I'm going to this wedding.

"Ah, I don't think so…"

"You and your boyfriend are busy?" Sebastian asks with a suspicious emphasis on the word boyfriend. Does he not believe me? Does he think I'd lie about this? I mean, I am, but he doesn't need to know that. Gosh, Sebastian is such a jerk.

I take a big sip of my wine to stall for time before finally answering, "I guess I can see if he's free?"

"Excellent. I'll put you and your plus one as a yes."

"Ah, wait…," I say, trying to pull back.

"I'll email you the details," Sebastian soldiers on. "Lilly, I can't wait to see you then. And meet this soul mate of yours. This will be a nice way for the two of you to celebrate Valentine's Day. At a wedding!"

"Ah, OK," I reply, dumbstruck and bewildered by this turn of events.

"I'll see you then, Lil. And I'm so happy you will be part of my special day." Sebastian hangs up the phone, and I sit and stare at my home screen. What have I done?

CHAPTER 19

"A MY?" I YELL THE NEXT morning as I let myself in the unlocked front door of the Harlow house. "Are you here? It's an emergency!" Since waking up to an email from Sebastian containing an invitation to his wedding, a wedding I agreed to attend with my imaginary boyfriend, I've been in a state of panic. After trying to calm my nerves with two cups of coffee, I hopped into Frankie, grateful again that I didn't pack my car keys in my now stolen handbag, and hightail it to Amy's place, hoping she'll help me find a way out of this situation.

"AMY?" I yell again as I walk down the front hallway.

"What?" comes a grumbled voice from the top of the stairs. "Lilly? How can you already be having a crisis this early on a Sunday morning?" she yawns as she walks down the stairs.

"Amy! This is serious. I need your help." I grab her arm to alert her to the urgency of my situation.

"OK, Lil. Let's get some coffee before we go any further," she says, giving me a proper look for the first time. "Though from what I can see, you don't need any more coffee."

I bounce on the balls of my feet, nervous energy spilling from me, and follow her to the kitchen.

As we enter the kitchen together, I blurt out, "I spoke to Seb last night!"

Amy's head shoots up, and she stares at me. "You did what?"

My attention is drawn from Amy when I spy Oliver sitting at the counter, eating a bowl of cereal. Frowning at me.

"Morning, Ol," I mutter as I walk towards where Amy is making the coffee, grabbing two cups.

"Are you sure you want another cup, Lil?" Amy asks.

"I'd take a coffee IV right about now, Amy. I'm in a world of pain."

"OK, back up," she says as the coffee is brewing. "Walk me through what happened. Did Seb call to get back together with you?"

I note Oliver is watching this interaction, and I turn my back to him.

"No, that's not the issue here. And even if he wanted to get me back, that ship has sailed and shipwrecked on a coral reef in a land far away."

"So what's the issue, then?" Amy probes, pouring the coffee into both our cups. I take a grateful sip from mine, eyeing Oliver, wishing he weren't around to hear this conversation.

"It started off fine, until he told me he'd broken up with me all those months ago to get together with Sarah, a friend from his work...," I start.

"He said what?" Amy interrupts while Oliver looks on, his jaw clenched in a way that suggests he's angry.

"Yes. And there's more. He and Sarah are getting married!"

"What?" Amy's obvious shock is making me feel a little better.

"Married?" Oliver asks, joining the conversation. "When?"

"In two weeks! Valentine's Day."

"In two weeks? Valentine's Day?" Amy parrots back, unable to comprehend what I'm telling her.

"And that's not the worst part. He invited me to his wedding, and—"

"He did what? The nerve of him!" Amy shouts, angry on my behalf.

"Not the worst part," I mutter.

"It gets worse than that?" Oliver questions, looking worried.

"I kind of did something stupid. I didn't mean to. I had had some wine, and before I knew it, I had I told him I was in a relationship, you know, to…"

"Save face," Amy finishes for me.

"Exactly!" I reply, glad she and I are on the same page.

"And that's bad because?" Oliver prompts.

"It's bad because I somehow agreed to go to his stupid wedding and bring my non-existent boyfriend with me." As silence follows this, I add, "And that's the worst part!"

"So let me get this straight. Your loser ex-boyfriend calls you out of the blue to tell you he's marrying the woman he left you for. And you agreed to attend his wedding with your made-up boyfriend?" Amy summarises.

"Yes," I say. "And that's why I'm here on a Sunday morning, in crisis mode. Help me," I add with a pathetic whimper.

Amy sips her coffee while she mulls this over as I watch Oliver from the corner of my eye. He appears to be deep in thought, his breakfast cereal going soggy on the counter in front of him.

"Well," Amy says with finality. "You just need to get a boyfriend before then."

"That's genius," I say, sarcasm coating my voice. "Why didn't I think of that?"

Amy laughs and says, "He doesn't have to be amazing; he just needs to be real."

I walk over to the couch in the adjacent living room, flop down onto it—covering my face with a cushion—and let out a groan.

"This isn't a solution. I don't have any options, good or bad, at the moment. It's not like I can call Grant 2.0 and ask him to come with me."

"Definitely not," Oliver says in a loud voice from the kitchen.

"It's that, or you have to tell Seb you can't go. Maybe we can come up with a good excuse?"

I think about what Amy has just suggested and again run through ideas in my head of ways to get out of this. But each time I picture telling Sebastian I won't be attending, I can see his smug face fill up with fake sympathy for poor, lonely Lilly, and my pride won't let me go there.

I look up as Amy joins me on the couch and say in a hopeful voice, "Do you think Harry Styles is available two weeks from today?"

Amy laughs as a look crosses her face.

"What?" I ask. "What are you thinking?"

She glances back towards the living room door, where Oliver is now leaning, watching this all unfold.

"Why don't you take Oliver with you?"

"Uh? What?" I exclaim. Amy has lost her mind.

"Me?" Oliver says at the same time.

"Yes, you can go with Lilly. As her pretend date." Her face lights up with pride like she has solved all the world's problems. "You have to admit, Lil, Oliver looks a bit like Harry Styles," she adds.

I stare at Oliver, who does look a lot like the aforementioned Mr Styles. "As much as I appreciate you offering your brother to me," I say, confused as I look at Oliver, who doesn't appear to be upset by the suggestion, "I don't think Emma would like this idea very much."

Silence follows this, with Amy biting her lip and glancing towards Oliver, who is now looking at the ground.

"What? What did I say?" I ask.

"Oliver and Emma broke up on Friday," Amy tells me in a quiet voice.

Shocked at this new piece of information, I glance at Oliver to gauge how upset he is by this recent development. He looks up at me and meets my eyes, not appearing to be heartbroken.

"I'm so sorry, Ol. I obviously didn't know. Are you OK? Do you need a hug?" I ask, wanting to make him feel better.

"I'm fine, thanks, Lil. It was a long time coming." Ever the stoic, Oliver stands up from his spot against the door frame and walks further into the room. After he takes a seat in the armchair across from me, he leans forward with his arms on his knees and says, "If you need me, I can pretend to be your boyfriend."

Unable to believe my ears, still shocked by the breakup announcement, I backtrack a bit.

"But you and Emma just broke up. What if she has a change of heart and then she learns you're going out with me, pretending, of course..."

"Lil, Oliver broke up with her. Not the other way around," Amy tells me almost proudly. "So there's no chance of them getting back together. Right, Ol?"

Oliver gives me a searching look, then answers, "That's right, we're done. And I'm free if you need me to be your date."

Buoyed by the fact that Oliver is now single and offering me a solution to my Sebastian problem, I tell him with a touch of hesitation, "It's a full weekend event. We'd need to be away for both Friday and Saturday nights."

"That sounds OK to me," Oliver says, not looking at all concerned.

"Are you sure? This is a lot to ask."

"No, it's not," Amy butts in. "He's happy to do it. You'd help him out if he needed it, right?"

"Of course," I say, and I mean it. I'd do anything for Oliver.

"Then it's settled. Lilly crisis averted. Now can I go back to bed? I have a late shift tonight with the douche bag Lucas, and I need all my energy to get through it." She gets up and gives me a hug. "Love you, Lilly Bug." And with a yawn, she heads up to bed.

I look at Oliver, who has been watching me this whole time, and ask again, "Are you sure you want to do this? It's going to take up your entire weekend. Don't you usually spend your weekend working? Or exercising? Or both?" I ask, giving him an out should he change his mind.

"Don't worry about me, Lilly. My work can wait. You're more important. I'm happy to play the role of your adoring boyfriend," he adds with a small smile while I blush on the inside at the sentiment behind what he has just said to me. Oliver willing to put aside work for me? It's unheard of.

"Just send me through the details, and we can organise from there." Ever the pragmatist, Oliver is focusing on the logistics, while I'm trying to calm my internal reaction to the idea of dating Oliver, even if it is only pretend.

"OK, will do. I'll sort out everything from my end, the hotel and stuff," I say, now focused on everything that needs to get done, including finding the perfect revenge dress—you know, the important stuff. "I'll email you what you need to know, and we can go from there."

Oliver nods.

"If you're sure?" I ask one last time, giving him a final chance to change his mind.

"I have never been surer of anything. Lilly Hamilton, it will be my honour to be your pretend boyfriend."

And with that, I fall for him just a little more.

CHAPTER 20

Lilly

A S PREDICTED, THE WORKING WEEK drags as I suffer through doing my actual job—you know, answering phone calls, filing papers, and of course, avoiding the wandering hands of my unsubtle male colleagues. This place is getting more unbearable by the day. It's a good thing that I have many things at the moment vying for equal shares of attention in my life: my burgeoning business (the Love, Lilly Instagram page now has one hundred thousand followers and is growing daily), my quest to find the perfect dress to wear to the wedding (involving scouring online boutiques and their sale options), and the heart-warming knowledge that Oliver has agreed to be my pretend boyfriend in two weeks' time. Every time I think of him offering to be my adoring boyfriend, I have to rein in my overactive imagination.

"It's just pretend, Lilly," I have to keep repeating to myself, and no good can come from getting caught up in the moment and be-lieving it is real.

Today I decide to spend my lunchtime focusing on capitalising on my online popularity and continuing to find a way to turn it into cold, hard cash. Following Oliver's suggestions, now that I've had such an increase in my follower numbers, I agreed to do sponsored advertisements for several bigger companies for their products. Some include bakeware and cooking utensils, with the bonus being I get to keep their products for free. And some have been for bigger items, like ovens and ThermoMixers, which I'm still trying to make work. The ability to generate a decent amount of money by posting sponsored ads and videos has boosted my chances of turning my hobby into a real business, and I get excited at the thought that this could lead to more and more lucrative deals for me in the future. And with my pop-up café opening in just six weeks' time, I'm feeling more positive that I could launch a successful Love, Lilly café soon. New Year's resolution to-do list items one and two—check!

In my downtime between answering emails, smiling at customers who come into the office, and being "decorative," I text with Amy, alternating between focusing on her heated relationship with Dr Lucas McHottie and my need to find a dress that will make Sebastian regret ever letting me go—and maybe get Oliver to notice me? Amy, true to form, is very encouraging of this quest and has been sending me links to every dress sale in a ten-kilometre radius, while I've been answering her rants about the very annoying (but very good-looking) doctor with angry face emojis and head-exploding-in-anger memes. This turns out to be a wonderful way to pass the time, and I as happen upon a funny angry-kitten GIF to send to Amy, I get a text from Oliver.

OLIVER: Hey, how're the plans for next weekend coming along? Need me to do anything to help?

This is interesting. It would seem that Oliver will not try to back out of this arrangement, as has been a fear of mine since I

RSVP'd to the wedding. Oliver isn't prone to doing crazy things, like pretend dating someone, so I had been waiting for him to come to his senses and bail out of the whole thing. With this message, I'm thinking that instead, he may actually be looking forward to accompanying me. No, that can't be right; he's just being Oliver, making sure I have things organised for the weekend and not leaving it to the last minute as I'm known to do.

LILLY: All good. Hotel booked. Now searching for a revenge dress.

OLIVER: A what?

LILLY: A revenge dress.

OLIVER: ???

LILLY: Oliver, you need to brush up on your pop culture references. A revenge dress is one that's worn to make an ex-boyfriend regret dumping you.

OLIVER: This is a thing?

LILLY: Yes, and I'm on a mission to find the perfect one.

OLIVER: You care what Sebastian thinks of you? You want him back?

OLIVER does not understand this. Clearly, he has never had to save face before.

LILLY: Being a typical man, you're missing the point. I DO NOT want him back or anywhere near me.

OLIVER: OK...

LILLY: I need to make sure I win the breakup.

OLIVER: You've lost me again.

I sigh to myself. This boy needs my help. Has he never watched a rom com before?

LILLY: I need to come out of this relationship looking the best. To those watching, he has moved on and is over me. He's getting married, and so far, that means he's winning. So, for me to win this breakup, I now must appear looking hot and make him feel bad about letting me go.

OLIVER: And he will do this? On his WEDDING day?

Hmmm, he may have a point. What am I trying to achieve here?

LILLY: Well, no, he probably won't notice me at all on his wedding day.

OLIVER: I wouldn't go that far. It's hard not to notice you, Lil. Revenge dress or not.

I feel my cheeks grow warm after reading this, and with a smile a mile long on my face, I reply: Regardless, the revenge dress is more about me and my ego.

OLIVER: Huh. I've learned something new today.

LILLY: You're welcome :)

OLIVER: Do I have a revenge dress equivalent? You know I just went through a breakup...

I feel bad about raving on about breakups when Oliver has just had his heart broken, so I pivot a bit.

LILLY: How are you doing, Ol? Hope you are OK?

OLIVER: I'm fine, really. Just need to find myself a revenge dress.

With a smile, I reply.

LILLY: Your revenge dress is just you living your best life. Emma will regret letting you go no matter what you wear.

The three dots appear and disappear several times before Oliver finally responds.

OLIVER: Thanks, Lilly. That means a lot.

OLIVER: Let me know if you need any help with your revenge dress shopping. Maybe I can help. Offer a male perspective?

LILLY: That would be amazing. You'd do that for me?

OLIVER: Of course. What's a fake boyfriend for? :)

OLIVER: How about I pick you up after work on Friday and we can go from there? Maybe have dinner afterwards? Discuss a game plan for the wedding?

My heart races at this.

LILLY: That sounds perfect.

OLIVER: Great. It's a date.

A date! Calm down, Lilly, it's not a real date.

When Friday finally arrives, I'm filled with impatience, waiting for the five o'clock bell to sound, metaphorically, of course. This place would never be cool enough to have an end-of-day bell. I dressed with extra care this morning, wearing a black pencil skirt and a fitted silk shirt with heels, knowing I will be seeing Oliver this evening, and have been receiving extra-special attention from the male species in the office as a result of this. When the slow hands of time finally click over to home time—I swear that minute hand has gone backwards more than a few times today—I glance up to see Oliver strolling into the office, looking like a snack in his business suit.

"Hey, Lil." His face lights up when he sees me. "I came straight from the office, so sorry for the business wear." He motions to the suit that looks like it is tailor made to fit his body.

"Don't be sorry," I say almost breathlessly. Have I ever seen Oliver in a suit like this before? Business casual, sure. Running clothes, swimwear, even pyjamas, yes, but never a charcoal suit paired with a black shirt that fits his body like a glove.

"You look nice," I add. I'm so lame!

Oliver smiles his special smile at me and comes over to give me a hug. At last—it's been too long since our last hug. Over Oliver's shoulder, I see Max, one of the senior real estate agents at the office, frowning at me.

"Lilly, who's this?" he asks as he walks over to where we're standing.

Oliver looks at Max, giving him a long overall glance, then turns back to me with a raised eyebrow.

"Max, this is Oliver," I tell him.

"Lilly's boyfriend," Oliver announces in a loud voice. My head snaps to Oliver. What's happening here?

"I didn't know Lilly had a boyfriend," Max responds, his gaze bouncing between the two of us. "Funny, she never mentioned you."

I stare at the face of this man who has made me uncomfortable for the entire time I've worked here, always asking me out and making me feel bad when I turn him down, and decide to pounce on this gift Oliver has given me, playing along.

I wrap my arm around Oliver's waist and lean my head against him. "Yes, Oliver and I have been together for years, Max. He's the reason I've been turning down your advances for the last twelve months," I add with glee.

Max's face turns a bright shade of red, while Oliver grunts in what he must think is a menacing tone, "You been bothering my girl?" To my ears, he sounds like someone attempting to mimic a Mafia boss. Poorly, I may add.

Nevertheless, Oliver's little manly display seems to have worked as I watch Max shift with discomfort.

"No, it's all in good fun. I just thought Lilly was lonely, that's all. No offence caused, I hope."

Oliver stands up taller, his six-feet-plus stature towering over the hobbit Max. "Hopefully you know now that Lilly is off limits. I don't want to hear any more about anyone bothering her. You got it?"

I tuck further into Oliver's arms, hiding my face in his chest to conceal my laughter, and once I have myself somewhat under control, I turn to see Max nodding, scurrying off back to his office.

"Thank you, sugarplum, for coming to my rescue yet again," I say to Oliver in a voice loud enough to carry around the entire office.

"No worries, my Lilly bean. No one gets to ask my girl out and get away with it."

I bite my lip to stop myself from laughing out loud and squeeze Oliver once more, turning to gather up my things.

"OK, lover bug, let's get going," I shout, having fun now, playing the role of doting girlfriend to a tee.

"I'll follow you wherever you go, honeybun," Oliver yells back, grinning at me. When he's like this, it's hard to believe that some people think Oliver is a bit of a stick in the mud. The man has a fun sense of humour.

We hold hands as we march out the front door, only allowing ourselves to laugh once we get in Oliver's car.

"You were brilliant in there, Ol!" I tell him once my laughter has died down a bit. "Now the word will spread that I have a big, tough boyfriend, and they'll leave me alone."

Oliver's amusement dies a little at this. "You shouldn't need a fake boyfriend to feel safe at work, Lil," he tells me, serious now. "You should feel safe to just be at work."

"I know. But this is a good temporary solution. And we now have some practice under our belts for the weekend!"

"True," Oliver concedes, still looking unconvinced.

As Oliver drives to the local shopping mall, I smile at him. "However, if we're going to make this fake relationship work, you need to work on your terms of endearment. Honey bun? Really? No self-respecting woman would allow herself to be called that."

Oliver shakes his head at me, laughing. "I'll work on it."

CHAPTER 21

Lilly

O NCE WE GET TO THE shopping mall, I take Oliver into the first dress store I see, hoping to get this part of the evening over and done with so we can get dinner and make our fake relationship plan. We step into what looks like a not-so-fancy, and therefore not-so-expensive, store, and I look around, trying to find something that catches my eye. Oliver, for his part, does not look bored, following close behind me and offering his opinion on any option I stop at.

With an arm full of potential outfits, I head to the fitting rooms, where I begin the laborious task of trying on dresses. This is the part of shopping that I hate the most. I struggle out of my fancy but oh-so-tight work outfit and try on option one: a fitted black dress. It has a classic silhouette, with a deep V neckline, that also hugs my hips and flares at the bottom, mermaid style. I have to take small steps, like a penguin as allowed by the design of the dress, and make my way out of the dressing room.

"What do you think?" I ask Oliver, gesturing to my dress with a flourish.

Oliver, who is sitting and scrolling through his phone, looks up and then stands. His eyes flare as he takes a step towards me. "Wow."

"You think?" I ask, not sold on this dress, craning my head around and trying to see the back of the dress in the mirror. "It's not too tight?"

Oliver swallows hard and shakes his head. "No, it's just right."

"Huh. Well, it's not comfortable at all, and I won't be able to sit, walk, or breathe in it all night, so I'm thinking no." After small stepping it back to the dressing room, I take off dress number one and attempt to get into dress number two. This one is a deep-red colour with a fitted bodice and off-the-shoulder straps, similar to the dress Julia Roberts wears in Pretty Woman. I have difficulty with the zip, so I back out of the dressing room, saying, "Hey Ol, can you help me with the zip?"

When Oliver doesn't reply, I look to see him in the mirror. He's standing behind me, staring at my bare back, hands in his pockets. Just staring.

"Ol?" I say again. "A little help?"

Oliver clears his throat, does the zip up, and stumbles as he backs away from me.

"What do we think of this one?" I ask now. "Revenge-y enough?"

Oliver looks at me with a small frown between his brows. "You look beautiful in this one too."

His voice is almost sad as he says this, and he sighs, his shoulders slumped.

With mild curiosity, I ask, "Why do you sound unhappy about this?"

"I don't think I thought this shopping excursion through very well," he says, almost like he's talking to himself. "I didn't think about what you'd look like in all these dresses."

Is Oliver maybe trying to tell me he's bored and has had enough of shopping without being rude? I decide to give him an out and cut our shopping trip short.

"I think I'm done trying on dresses today, anyway." I tell him. "Can you unzip me, and we can get some dinner?"

With a pained look—gosh, he must be so bored—Oliver steps closer and pulls on the zip. I feel his warm hands on my bare back and agree with him. Maybe this shopping together wasn't a great idea after all.

"You're all set," Oliver says at last.

"Thanks, I'll just take this off, and we can be on our way."

"I'll wait for you outside," he says, his voice again strained. "No rush."

I shake my head at how weird Oliver is behaving and take the red dress off before getting back into my work clothes, ones I can breathe in. I hand over the unwanted outfits to the sales assistant and thank her for her help.

"No worries," she says. "And girl, your man is fine." She points to where Oliver is standing waiting for me.

"Don't I know it!" I reply with a smile as I leave the store.

After looking around for a short while, we find a suitable place to have dinner. We find a table, and Oliver and I take a seat, each grabbing a menu. To get the evening back on track, I start a running commentary of my potential meal choices:

"I could have the risotto dish, but I had risotto the night I was out with Grant 2.0, and ugh, that now has bad associations, and I really should try something different. Ooh, seafood! Do I feel like seafood today? Pasta? Yes, definitely pasta! Oh, but there's pizza, and I love pizza. This is too difficult!" I finish up, having worked hard and made no decisions.

Oliver laughs, seeming to enjoy my antics. "Why don't we order two dishes and share? Then you can have pasta and pizza."

Sigh, why does he have to be so perfect all the time?

"But do you want either pasta or pizza?" I ask.

Oliver shrugs. "I don't really care. If this makes you happy, let's do it." He grabs the attention of the waitress and orders the pasta and the pizza with extra plates for sharing.

"Happy now?" he asks.

"Absolutely. Can I keep you as my fake boyfriend forever?"

The smile on Oliver's face fades, and I realise what I just said.

"Only kidding!" I hasten to tell him. "I know this is a one-time offer and that we'll be back to friends after the wedding. Not that we have to stop being friends while we're at the wedding. Oh, you know what I mean..." I trail off, wringing my hands and feeling awkward.

"I know what you mean, Lil. And don't worry, no matter what happens, we'll always be friends," he reassures me.

I settle back in my seat, feeling better, and look at him. I could stare at his face all day. He's so handsome.

"So what's the plan for the weekend?" Oliver asks, ever the pragmatist.

"It shouldn't be too difficult. I figure we just keep a low profile, don't draw too much attention to ourselves, and leave at the earliest opportunity."

"And what about our backstory? Should anyone ask?"

"Hmmm, we can keep it simple. We've been friends forever, then it turns out you have been secretly pining for me and finally found the nerve to ask me out, and here we are?" I offer.

Oliver doesn't respond straight away, instead stares at me with a strange intensity until I start to squirm in my seat.

"You don't think that will work? It's not believable enough?" I ask.

Oliver looks away for a moment before finally saying, "Sounds real enough to me."

Before I can delve into that any deeper, the waitress puts our food on the table, and I'm distracted by the deliciousness in front of me.

"Hmm, so good," I say as I alternate between bites of pizza and pasta.

Once full, I lean back in my seat and pat my belly with a happy grin.

"Satisfied now?" Oliver asks with an indulgent smile.

"Yes, but there's always room for more happiness..."

"Dessert?" Oliver guesses correctly.

"Shall we?"

"Of course," Oliver says, picking up the menu again. "What do you feel like?"

After we've placed our dessert orders, Oliver brings us back to the task at hand, a crash course in how to fake date your best friend. We pick up from where we left off, and he summarises. "So we were friends who are now lovers," he says, causing me to blush to the tips of my ears, "and we're madly in love and can't keep our hands off each other?"

As Oliver says the words madly in love, it's like a bomb explodes in my mind, and I'm blinded by the realisation that what Oliver is saying is true. For me. Not the part about being lovers, but the being-in-love part? That is true. I am so in love with Oliver that I can't even see straight. How has it taken me so long to work this out? I've always been OK with the small crush I have on him. It has always been there, a part of me, like another limb. It has even been a big enough deal in my life to make the number four spot on my New Year's resolution to-do list, but honest-to-goodness love? I never considered it. I look at Oliver now, at his handsome and oh-so-familiar face, with dimples I can drown in, and my heart gives a painful squeeze. Of course I love him. I have always loved him. And now, with this knowledge, I have to play the role of his pretend girlfriend for a weekend to save face for a useless ex-boyfriend I've never loved. What have I done? This is so much more complicated now.

At seeing what must be my stricken expression, Oliver rushes to say, "We don't have to be all over each other, Lilly. I was just using it as an example."

I take a big sip of water, choking as it goes down the wrong way, and finally gasp, "No, it's fine. It's all good. The plan is solid. No need to talk about it anymore."

"But…" Oliver goes to say something more, still looking at me with concern.

"Oh, look, our dessert is here." I grab hold of a plate of tiramisu like it's a lifeline out of this conversation. "Let's dig in!" I add with forced enthusiasm.

Oliver gives me a strange look but does as I say, and we both finish our dessert in silence. Once we settle the bill—Oliver insisting on paying, saying it's his "duty as my boyfriend to pay for my dinner"—we walk to Oliver's car.

"Are you sure you're OK, Lil? Is it the fact that Sebastian is getting married that has you a bit upset?" Oliver asks with quiet compassion.

"No, Ol. I couldn't care any less about Seb. I guess maybe I'm just tired? Shopping is like a cardio workout for me," I offer as a lame excuse.

"OK, well, let's get you home to bed." He blushes a bit, perhaps at the implications of his words. "To your bed, on your own, by yourself," he adds in a rush.

With some of my composure restored, I can laugh a little at his discomfort. Squeezing his arm, I say, "Yes, let's get me to my bed, all alone, by myself."

Oliver joins me with a little laugh, and the weird tension that has been building since my life-altering revelation dissipates somewhat. Until I remember that I now know I'm in love with my friend, and I have no clue what I'm going to do about it.

CHAPTER 22

Oliver

AFTER I DROP LILLY BACK at her apartment, I drive home, lost in thought about the time we just spent together. I was clearly not thinking straight when I offered to go dress shopping with Lilly, not anticipating how she would actually look in all the revenge dress candidates. My stomach tightens as I picture Lilly in those dresses. She's so gorgeous. The preview of what she's going to look like at the wedding, when she'll be all glammed up, is making me think I'm going to have a lot of trouble keeping my hands to myself this weekend. Though, I'm playing the role of her fake boyfriend, so maybe my hands can have a bit more freedom than they're usually allowed around Lilly. I smile at this thought, grateful again that Amy proposed this little fake-dating plan for the two of us.

As I drive, I think about the strange way Lilly was acting towards the end of dinner. I wonder if she is in fact feeling more upset about the Sebastian breakup and subsequent wedding than she's letting on. I will need to make sure I'm extra sensitive to this over the weekend in case she needs me to comfort her. As a pretend boyfriend, of course.

I also reluctantly think about how and when I'm going to make up for all these hours I'm taking off when I should be working. Right now is a critical time in my career, with that upcoming promotion in sight, and yet ever since I agreed to be Lilly's fake boyfriend, I can't seem to find the enthusiasm to spend all my extracurricular hours working. It's becoming apparent that being with Lilly is taking centre stage in my life, something I always feared would happen.

As I approach my street, almost home, my phone rings, and I see Dale is calling me. I answer him, using my Bluetooth device for safety reasons, of course.

"Hey, man, what are you up to?" Dale asks.

"Nothing much. I just dropped Lilly off at her apartment and am heading home," I tell him with some reluctance. Dale has been like a dog with a bone when it comes to me and Lilly.

True to form, Dale jumps on this bit of information. "Excellent news. So you finally asked her out?"

"Not exactly." I fill Dale in on the upcoming plans to be Lilly's pretend boyfriend at her ex-boyfriend's weekend wedding.

"So you see? It's a foolproof plan. A way to show Lilly that we're good together. With no pressure."

Ever direct, Dale tells me, "You have got the fool bit right. Man, this sounds like a recipe for disaster. And it sounds like something a man like you would never take part in. Not in a million years."

Dale is right about this one thing. My life is so structured, filled with plans and plans to make plans, that the thought of my spending a weekend at the wedding of two complete strangers, play-acting as Lilly's boyfriend, is ludicrous. However, I know in my gut that if Lilly and I have any chance of being something more than friends, this is the step I have to take. So I shake my head at him, even though I know he can't see me.

"It will be a way to take baby steps with Lilly. To show her what sort of boyfriend I can be. And finally get me out of the friend zone."

"Wouldn't it be easier to just ask her out?"

Dale does not understand what I'm up against. A lifetime of being Lilly's best friend.

"No, because if I make a move and Lilly doesn't feel the same, it could all blow up in my face. Trust me, this is the way to go."

"OK, I can't wait to hear how this all plays out when it's over."

I arrive home and use this as an opportunity to say goodbye to the pessimistic energy of Dale, and I think to myself, This is definitely the best path forward.

Now I just need to work on how I'm going to spend the weekend pretending that my real feelings for Lilly are actually fake. With this circular logic floating around my head, wondering if this is what it always feels like in Lilly's mind, I grin to myself. This weekend cannot come fast enough.

CHAPTER 23

Lilly

T HE NEXT DAY, I DO anything I can to keep my mind off Oliver and the realisation that I'm a lovesick fool over him. So lovesick that I could write a country album right now, one about love realised too late, love found and lost. How did I let this happen? I think to myself as I clean my apartment from top to bottom, doing all the chores I normally put off, to keep my mind occupied. After the place is spotless, I then spend hours stress baking all my favourite foods, cupcakes, muffins, and three banana cakes to put in the freezer for another day. Once that's done, I flop onto the couch and try to distract myself by binge watching my favourite comfort show, The Great British Bake Off, but even the soothing tone of the baking judge extraordinaire, Paul Hollywood, can't get my mind off what I've discovered. So, before I go to bed, I cave and send a text to Amy.

LILLY: SOS! Help! Shopping for revenge dress and girl talk needed!

Amy replies with a few emojis of hearts and talking faces and tells me she'll come to my place in the morning for a stint of power shopping followed by a much-needed girl talk session. With this in place, I feel comforted enough to unwind, and after some tossing and turning, I fall into an Oliver-dream-filled sleep.

Amy arrives the next morning, armed with Instagram pages pinned with dresses she vows will look "perfect" on me, and bottles of wine for later to help us get through our impromptu therapy session.

"You're the best!" I tell her, giving her a big hug at my front door.

"I know," she says without a shred of modesty. "You'd be lost without me," she adds with a cheeky grin. "Now let's get you a revenge dress so sexy it will knock Sebastian's ugly socks off!" She was never a fan of Sebastian, and it would seem that even his socks can't escape her wrath.

Already feeling better, I grab my bag and put on some comfortable shoes, knowing Amy will extract the most shopping time as possible out of this excursion and wanting to avoid sore feet and blisters at all costs.

Once at the shops, Amy takes charge, dragging me in and out of stores until we finally find "the one." The Perfect Dress. A dress so beautiful that just looking at it, I know I have to make it mine. And then once I have it on my body, I don't want to take it off; it fits me like a glove. So much so that it feels like someone made the dress with me specifically in mind. When I come out of the dressing room, Amy squeals and claps, letting me know she agrees.

"You look amazing, Lil," she gushes, making me spin around so she can see the back. "Please tell me you love this one."

As she takes pictures of me to send to Madi and Sammi, who are waiting to give their fashion opinions, I grin as I look at myself in the mirror, peering around to see the dress from all angles. I picture Oliver's face when he sees me in the dress and know that I'd sell a kidney, if need be, to make it mine.

I hand over my credit card, closing my eyes and trying to ignore the ridiculous amount of money I'm spending, and force myself to think of it as an investment instead. Every girl needs a dress like this once in her lifetime. For some, it's their wedding dress. For me, it's this one, which it would seem, costs about as much as a wedding dress.

By the look on Amy's face, I can tell she agrees. "The girls both give this dress a huge thumbs up." She shows me the chain of text messages filled with emojis of smiley faces with heart-shaped eyes.

"And remember, you work hard for your pay cheque, so you deserve this." When she sees the look I'm giving her, she revises her statement, "OK, well you work for your pay cheque. And at a horrible, dead-end job. You 100 percent deserve this." I agree with this sentiment, and with a lot of care, I grab my precious cargo, dragging Amy out of the store before she can even think of looking at any shoes, handbags, or jewellery.

Once home, I hang the dress in my closet, spending a few seconds just stroking the fabric with my fingertips, before I settle on the couch with Amy. While I was busy doing this, Amy took it upon herself to put out a platter of my latest baked creations and has poured us each a glass of wine. Once comfortable, she spears me with a look and says, "OK, talk."

I take a deep breath and blurt out, "I think I'm in love with Oliver!"

Amy blinks at me, her wine glass paused halfway to her lips. "And?"

"What do you mean, and?" I say in a huff. How can she not see how monumental this discovery is for me? Mind-blowingly monumental.

"Well, Lilly, I thought you were going to confess something to me I didn't already know."

Dumbfounded, I stare at her for a moment, shoving a cupcake in my mouth while Amy chews on her cookie, looking at me thoughtfully.

"You know?" I ask after taking a minute to compose myself.

"Lilly, we all know. Madi, Sammi, and I talk about it all the time! You've been in love with Oliver since you were sixteen years old. We always thought you knew and just didn't want to talk about it. How could you not know?"

When I just stare at her, she continues, "I just want to know if you're finally going to do something about it?"

"What?" I squeak. "Back up. What are you saying?"

"Lil, Oliver has always been the guy for you. Think about it: you've always compared all your boyfriends to him and found them lacking," she continues. "And you've always been so funny about his girlfriends."

"You have to admit they've all been pretty bad," I interrupt.

"I know," she agrees. And then she drops the bombshell. "And Oliver has always had a thing for you too."

I lean forward, getting very close to Amy's face, and say in a loud voice, "What are you talking about?"

Amy sighs. "For two seemingly intelligent people, you're pretty dumb about this." When it looks like I'm going to explode, she continues, "Haven't you ever wondered why Oliver has hated every guy you have ever dated?"

"I never really thought about it," I admit. "Generally, I end up hating every guy I date as well."

Amy grins at me and nods in acknowledgment. "Well, Oliver has always been protective of you. Some may say almost possessively protective. Think about this: I'm his sister, and he couldn't care less who I date. And he never comments about the love lives of Madi or Sammi," she points out. "But with you, he has so many opinions, and none of them are positive."

I think about what Amy is saying, and it's true, Oliver has always been pretty vocal when it comes to my love life and has left Amy and the girls to make some pretty poor decisions about their own.

"That just means he trusts your judgments more than he trusts mine," I throw at her with a little triumphant jig.

"Maybe?" Amy replies, unconvinced. "But it's more than that. Take, for example, that time Seb broke up with you and left you up in the snow?" I nod for her to continue. "When I told Oliver what happened, he went berserk. He was worried and angry and had his keys ready and was in his car to get you before I could even get my shoes on."

"Wait! I thought Oliver came for me because you couldn't do it?"

"Lilly, Oliver didn't give me a choice. As soon as he heard you were by yourself and upset, he couldn't get to you fast enough. To make sure you were OK. It was very sweet, in an annoying way."

I take a minute to ponder this new information in silence as I pour us both some more wine. Could Oliver have feelings for me? Feelings beyond the protective-big-brother type?

Another thought enters my head. "OK, well how about the fact that his girlfriends are always my polar opposite? He has a type, and it isn't me!"

Amy shakes her head at me, disappointed. "That may be true. He does seem to gravitate to the well-organised but oh-so-boring girls. I've never been convinced that's who he wants to be with but more like who he thinks he should be with."

As I think about this, Amy adds, "And what about you, Lilly? Have you dated people the same as Oliver? Or have they all been like Seb? From what I've observed over the years, you tend to go for guys that are nothing like Oliver."

Stumped by this, I ask another question, "Why has he never asked me out?"

"Why haven't you ever asked him out?" she throws the question back at me. "You're both too scared to make a move and face potential rejection. Or ruin your friendship. So you both do nothing, date the wrong people, and generally make everything miserable for me."

"Sorry to make your life so terrible," I say in a voice that contains no amount of remorse. "So it wouldn't bother you if I was to be with Oliver?"

"Are you kidding me? You're already like my sister. This would just make it official," she says, almost bouncing up and down with excitement at the thought.

I know I need to calm her down and get the conversation back on track, so I tell her, "Slow down, Ames. I'm still not convinced you're right and that Ollie has feelings for me."

"But you're in love with him!" she repeats.

"I know," I say. "And apparently, so does everyone. Gosh, I hope Oliver doesn't know!" I add with a panicked look.

Amy gives me an adamant shake of her head. "No, he's just as clueless as you."

Great. Thanks, I think to myself.

"Now I need to figure out where to go from here," is what I say to Amy.

"You don't need to make any big moves right now. The beauty of this pretend relationship weekend you have coming up is that you can just test the waters. See if Oliver responds. See what it would be like to be with him that way? It may all happen naturally, and then you will know."

Once I agree this is in fact a good plan and that nothing more can be done about this now, I pack up some treats for Amy to take home to Oliver, give her a big hug filled with gratitude, and with Johnny as our escort, walk her to her car to say goodbye.

After Amy's departure, I clean up the leftover desserts and wine glasses and lie back down on my couch, trying to digest all that I learned tonight. Could it be true? Could Oliver have feelings for me? Whatever the truth is, this weekend cannot come fast enough.

CHAPTER 24

F RIDAY ARRIVES AT LAST, AND as I pack up my desk at work and log off my computer, my stomach is filled with butterflies. Unsure of what this weekend will bring, I'm excited to be spending so much one-on-one time with Oliver, pretending to be a couple no less. And testing out the waters of what could be a potential relationship. Just thinking about it fills me with equal measures of excitement and blind terror.

This past week, I've been in regular contact with Oliver. Every day, he has been alternating between calling me and texting me, sometimes spending hours on the phone well into the night, both of us missing sleep because of it. It's made me wonder where Oliver is finding the time to fit me in, given his already jam-packed work schedule. And this is making me think that there may be a teeny, tiny chance Amy is correct. Would Oliver dedicate so much of his precious time to someone he only sees as a friend? With this in my mind, I'm now seeing every interaction with Oliver through a different lens. When he sends me sweet messages, I wonder if they could mean something more. And then when my heart races every time he calls, I know I'm in big trouble.

After I get home from work—hooray—I finish packing and wait for Oliver to pick me up. I have packed some banana chocolate chip muffins for the two-hour drive ahead and have a road trip playlist ready to go. In true Oliver style, right on time, he knocks on my door, and when I answer, he looks so good I have to take a step back to stop from throwing myself at him. He's wearing blue jeans that fit him like a glove and a black polo shirt that hugs his biceps just right, and his hair is tousled in a way that makes me want to run my fingers through it. If this is how I'm feeling just looking at him for thirty seconds, this weekend is going to be a test of my self-control. I know I agreed with Amy to use this weekend to "test the relationship waters" with Oliver, but I don't think that involves jumping his bones the minute he walks in the door. A shame, really.

"Ready to go, Lil?" he asks, flashing his dimples at me.

"Yup," I reply. "And I have snacks!" I tell him, holding up my Tupperware container.

Oliver grabs my suitcase; and we head out the front door, with Oliver telling me as we leave to "lock the front door behind us," making me roll my eyes and stick my tongue out at him behind his back. Must he always think of me as incompetent?

"The GPS and Google Maps say it will take two hours to get there, even with some traffic," Oliver tells me as we head downstairs and towards where he parked his car. Of course Oliver has checked the travel times from two independent sources, just to be 100 percent sure. "So I think we should be able to get there and get settled before dark."

"Sounds good to me," I say, happy to leave the decision making up to him, waving to Johnny from my window.

As I settle into the front passenger seat, I watch Oliver put my suitcase in the car's trunk and give Johnny a timid wave. I smile at this small interaction and then plug my iPhone into his speaker system, ready to get this road trip off to a good start.

"What are you subjecting my ears to today?" Oliver asks as he starts up the car and heads away from my apartment building.

"Only the finest road trip tunes ever written." I reply, flashing him a big smile. "You just drive, and I'll be in charge of food and entertainment."

Oliver nods with a smile and grabs an offered muffin, groaning as he takes a bite, and we settle in for the drive ahead. The wedding is to be held in a large hotel in the seaside town of Sorrento, which is known for its sandy beaches and resort-style feel while only being a few hours' drive away from Melbourne. The hotel I've booked is the same one where the wedding is taking place, making for an easy weekend with everything on our doorstep. Having checked out reviews and pictures online, I'm looking forward to a little luxury this weekend.

While we drive, we make small talk, focused for the most part on my Love, Lilly Instagram success, with Oliver offering helpful suggestions for bolstering potential sponsorships and revenue, and the time passes by in a hurry, as it so often does when we're together. Oliver fills me in on gossip from his office, including a tidbit about one of his co-workers asking him out. He seems to think it's an amusing anecdote, while I grit my teeth and curse this unknown woman in my mind. Who is she to swoop in on the newly single, still broken-hearted Oliver, anyway?

When I can no longer hold back the question, I ask, "So are you going to go out with her?" I need to know the answer before the weekend can continue.

Oliver sends me a quick glance before looking back at the road. "No, I'm not interested in her. It was just a tricky situation, that's all. I let her down gently, but now I must see her every day at work, and we're friends, and it's a bit..." He pauses.

"Uncomfortable?" I finish for him.

"Yes, it's hard to have to be friends with someone when you've essentially rejected them."

These words reverberate around my head, with big flashing warning signs attached to them. Warning me against doing something stupid. Because despite what Amy may believe, if I were ever to act on these feelings I have for Oliver and he didn't reciprocate, what would become of our friendship? I'd rather have Oliver in my life, even if it's just as a friend, than to end up as someone he needs to avoid.

"It's too soon for you to be dating anyway, given that you and Emma just broke up. The next girl would end up being a rebound," I tell him, hoping to sound casual and not like my heart is hurting.

Oliver gives me another look, longer this time, and says nothing. We sit in silence for the next hour until we reach the Sorrento Resort and Spa, our home for the next few days.

After Oliver parks the car and grabs our bags, we make our way to reception to check in, when it dawns on me, finally, that we're going to be sharing a room. Just the two of us. And because I didn't think about this for more than two seconds when booking the room, I asked for one with a king-sized bed. Because I love the luxury of having a big bed all to myself. How did I manage to mess this up? One room, one bed, with Oliver. For two entire nights. And seriously, how is this only occurring to me now? When I look at Oliver from the sides of my eyes, I note that he doesn't seem at all perturbed, because he's a logical human being who's clearly anticipated this situation, given that we're here as a "couple" this weekend.

"As you are guests of the wedding party, we have reserved you a deluxe room, on the fourth floor with a view of the ocean. As requested, it's a room with a king-sized bed," the receptionist tells us, looking at Oliver the whole time with heart shapes in her eyes while I groan internally. Damn me and my need to have a big bed! I look at Oliver to see if he is at all uncomfortable with sharing a bed, and when he looks at me with a smile and a wink, I decide to not explore the option of requesting a room with separate beds. I want to avoid anyone figuring out that we're not really a couple, and I also want to stop this receptionist lady from flirting with my pretend boyfriend. Even as I stand here, she's running through all the services the hotel has to offer, which if her sultry voice is anything to go by, includes a personal massage for Oliver and Oliver alone.

"Thank you," I cut in, my tone aggressive. Can she not see that he's here with me? "We will just get our key and be on our way," I add, looking between the two of us. We.

Oliver looks at me with a small laugh as he shakes his head. It's like he can read my inner monologue and finds it all very amusing.

"The lifts are just through that way," the reception lady tells us, eyes still glued to Oliver, smiling at him, not sparing me a glance. "Please call me if you need anything. Anything at all."

Oliver gives her a dismissive glance and puts his arm around my shoulder, guiding us away.

"What's her problem?" I grumble as we walk away. "Am I wearing my invisibility cloak today? How dare she flirt with you while I'm standing right there? And stop laughing, it's not funny!" I add when he continues to look at me with amusement.

"Don't even worry about her, Lil. I'm not giving her a second thought."

I feel reassured by this, opening the door to our hotel room and stopping short at the sight of the king-sized bed in the middle of the room. Like the proverbial elephant in the room but only bigger. I creep into the room, looking with determination anywhere except for at Oliver and the bed. I curse myself again for not having thought about this at all. Oliver and I will be sharing a bed. Sharing. A. Bed.

I clear my throat and look at Oliver, who is also looking anywhere but at me and the bed. He walks over to the window to take in the view, while I sidestep around the elephant bed, walking up to the small desk where there is a folder with our names on it. Grateful for the distraction, I open it to find a full itinerary printed of the activities for the next two days.

"Brunch on the lawn at 10:00 a.m. tomorrow," I read out loud as Oliver gets our suitcases and wheels them further into the room, setting them down next to the closet. "Beach activities, followed by a picnic. And a joint bachelor-and-bachelorette party tomorrow night." I groan, looking at the long list of things we will have to endure over the weekend. So much for keeping a low profile, making a brief appearance at the wedding, and then disappearing.

"Sounds like fun," Oliver says, reading over my shoulder. "Beach volleyball and tug of war? I'm up for it."

"Of course you are," I reply. "You're always happy to get out and be active. What's so wrong with a spa day, followed by room service in our robes?"

"We can do the room service tonight," Oliver offers.

"Really?" I love room service. "You wouldn't rather go out?"

"I'm tired from the drive, and it's been a long week. Why don't we order in and watch a movie on Netflix?"

I think this sounds like pure bliss, so I grab the in-service menu and begin perusing the options.

"We should get dessert as well," I mutter as I try to decide between steak and lobster.

"We can get whatever you want, Lilly."

Looking up, I see Oliver watching me with an indulgent smile on his face, and I melt just a little. Why must he always be so good to me?

Two hours later, after ordering both the steak and the lobster (at Oliver's insistence, so we can each try a bit of both) and a slice of heavenly chocolate cheesecake to top off the night, Oliver and I are sitting on the bed, leaning back, laughing at some silly comedy movie on the TV. Well, Oliver is watching it. Me? Well, I'm not paying any attention to what's on the screen in front of me, too focused on the man beside me. Too busy taking in his divine scent. And the feel of his arm when it brushes against mine. The night ahead is going to be torture for me. I watch Oliver from the corner of my eye, and he looks so comfortable, not affected at all by my nearness. He's not concerned in the slightest at the thought of sleeping next to me. Amy has this all wrong; Oliver clearly has no romantic feelings for me.

"Hey, Lil, the movie is over." Oliver says, breaking me out of my internal monologue. "Do you want to use the bathroom first? We probably should get some sleep to prepare for the big day they have in store for us tomorrow."

"You go first," I offer, trying to gather my scattered thoughts. How can he be so unaffected by this situation?

While Oliver is in the bathroom, I send a frantic text to the girls, apprising them of the situation. True to form, not a single one of them is at all helpful, sending back smiley faces, eggplant emojis, and memes of people kissing. I need to get new friends.

"Bathroom is free." I look up from my phone to see a fresh-out-of-the-shower, oh-so-adorable Oliver standing before me in a pair of grey sweatpants and nothing else. As I look at his chest and sculpted abs, I gulp, and gathering up my bag, I rush into the bathroom, locking the door behind me. For Oliver's safety, not mine.

After a freezing-cold shower and several stern talkings to, I let myself out of the bathroom and see Oliver already in bed. He looks amazing with the light bouncing off his smooth chest. I hurry to put my clothes away and make my way towards the bed, stopping when I see Oliver is staring at me with a fierce expression on his face. As I follow his gaze downward, I realise I'm wearing his T-shirt and a tiny pair of night shorts. He's not to know that I've taken to wearing his T-shirt to bed almost every night, and not having anticipated sharing a room with Oliver—so stupid—I packed this to wear this weekend.

"You did say I could keep it," I remind him, trying to break the weird tension in the room.

Oliver says nothing, continuing to stare at me. He swallows hard, his Adam's apple bobbing up and down, then he looks away to stare hard at the ceiling.

I creep into the bed and try to think of something to say to make this less uncomfortable. As I slide under the blanket, as close to the edge as possible, I joke, "Well, we haven't done this before."

"Done this?" Oliver asks in a distracted voice, still staring at the roof.

"Umm, slept in the same bed."

"I seem to remember many a night sharing a bed with you, Lilly," Oliver offers.

"This isn't exactly a sleeping bag in a tent in the woods, now is it?" I say with a relieved laugh. "And we aren't eight years old either."

Oliver looks over at me, his jaw clenching, taking in my face peeking out from under the blanket, before his gaze traces the outline of my body. "No, we certainly aren't kids anymore."

"This will be fine, won't it, Ollie? We can do this. I promise to keep to my side of the bed and not hog the blanket," I say, again trying to lighten the mood.

"You know you will be safe here in this bed with me, don't you, Lil?" Oliver asks with a look of sudden concern.

"Of course! I know you wouldn't try to make a move on me, that you don't see me that way. We're just two friends camping out together again."

Oliver's face is filled with doubt, and after looking at me for a long moment, he lets out a heavy sigh. He rolls over to turn off his lamp and says, "Goodnight, Lilly. Sweet dreams."

As I turn away from Oliver to face the wall, I think to myself, This is going to be a long night.

CHAPTER 25

Lilly

I WAKE UP TO A feeling of utter contentment and snuggle closer to the source of the nearby warmth, taking in a deep breath, filling my lungs with that smell, that one that always makes me think of Oliver. Oliver! As I emerge from unconsciousness, I realise that at some point during the night, I migrated across the bed towards Oliver, and that's where I am now, wrapped around him, like a koala bear hugging a tree. My arm is thrown over his waist, holding on tightly, and my leg is hooked around both of his. I'm pressed so close to his body I can't see where I end and he begins.

How did this happen? OK, stupid question. This happened because my body physically cannot stay away from his, but how has he not extricated himself from me? I look up from where my head is nuzzling into his chest and let out a relieved breath when I see Oliver is still asleep. There's still time to salvage this situation. I just need to get back to my side of the bed without waking him up. As gently as I can, I take my leg off his and move away from his warm body, when he murmurs in his sleep, frowning, and pulls me back. Great. Now what? It would seem that Oliver's sleeping form is enjoying this little impromptu cuddle, but I doubt a conscious Oliver would feel the same. Not wanting the day to start off on an awkward note, I try again to get out of this lovely but oh-so-inappropriate embrace. I think back to one of my favourite episodes of Friends, the one where Ross tells Chandler how to get out of spooning Janice all night ("hug for her, roll for me"), and I pull Oliver closer for a tight squeeze, then roll away from him in one swift motion. Quick as a cat. And roll straight off the bed.

"Ouch!"

"Lilly?" Oliver speaks up, his voice rough with sleep. "What happened? Are you OK?"

I poke my head up from where I'm now sitting on the floor next to the bed and flash a thumbs up. I'm such a dork.

"All good here. Just some gymnastics to start the day." What? What did I just say? "Did you sleep well?" I ask, changing the subject.

Oliver yawns and stretches his arms above his head, exposing an expanse of tanned chest, while I force myself to look away in an effort to not drool over him first thing in the morning.

"That was the best sleep I've had in years." He gives me a contemplative look.

"Must be the sea air," I say as I get up and head to the bathroom, wondering if Oliver remembers our night-time cuddle.

"I'm going to get ready for the day," I add as I step into the bathroom. "Lots of activities to keep us busy. Rise and shine, early bird catches the worm, and all that," I ramble on, no longer in control of what's coming out of my mouth.

I hear Oliver chuckling as I close the door and hurry through my morning routine. After brushing my teeth, I attempt to get my hair in order, embarrassed that Oliver has seen me with bed hair. After plaiting my hair into two braids, I dress in a white bikini (one with more coverage than the last time Oliver and I went swimming together), throw on a short sundress in a bright shade of turquoise that matches my eyes, and smother my face with sunscreen. Unlike Oliver with his beautiful olive skin, I burn at the slightest hint of sunshine, and I don't want to attend the wedding tomorrow looking like a boiled lobster.

As I exit the bathroom, I see Oliver has already dressed for the day. He looks amazing, as per usual, in blue, red, and white shorts and another polo shirt that's doing great things for all his muscles. I stand and stare at him for a beat, unable to stop my gaze from running over him. I notice Oliver is doing the same to me, making me flush and squeak, "Bathroom's free." After this embarrassing display, I let Oliver pass by and attempt to busy myself by filling my beach bag with the day's essentials. Phone, sunscreen, hat, water bottle. All packed and good to go.

Once Oliver has finished getting ready, I stop him before we leave the room.

"Are we set on the game plan?" I ask, reminding us of both of the reason he's here with me. "Are you ready to play the part of my adoring boyfriend? To help my ego and save me a lifetime of humiliation?" I add with a touch of dramatics.

Oliver laughs and grabs my hand as we leave the room. "I've been ready for this for a long time, Lilly."

Huh? That shuts me up as we make our way down to reception, where we are meeting the wedding crew for the day.

"Lilly!" I look up to see Sebastian and who I assume is his fiancée moving towards us as we exit the elevator. "I'm so glad you're here. I wasn't sure you'd turn up," he adds, which is weird given I RSVP'd saying I'd be there. Maybe-Sarah is looking at me up and down with a vacant smile on her face, and I plaster a fake smile on my own.

"You must be Sarah? It's so nice to meet you. Thanks for inviting us to join in your special day."

"Oh, sure, no worries, it's all good," Sarah says in a high-pitched voice, sounding like she may be drunk already. Or maybe she's just always a little vague?

Feeling awkward, I pull Oliver closer to me and introduce him, "Seb, Sarah, this is Oliver. My boyfriend."

Oliver flashes his friendly, dimpled-filled smile, and I relax a bit. Just knowing he's here to have my back is making this conversation almost bearable.

"Nice to meet you both. I echo Lilly over here and thank you for your kind invitation to join you this weekend."

Sarah beams at Oliver, and for unknown reasons, decides to give him a sloppy hug. She must be charmed by Oliver and his dimples, while in contrast to this, Sebastian looks at him with open hostility.

"Oliver?" Sebastian says. "You look familiar. Aren't you the older brother of Lilly's best friend? Annie?"

"Amy," we both correct him, me feeling pretty annoyed given that Sebastian and I were a couple for over four months and friends for around six months before that, and he couldn't even recall the name of my best friend.

"So how long have you two been a couple?" Sebastian continues, sounding somewhat suspicious.

"Oh, almost a year," I say, pretending to do the relationship maths. "Probably as long as you two have been together," I add, pointing between Sarah and Sebastian.

"You obviously weren't very heartbroken then, when we broke up. To move on so quickly," Sebastian has the nerve to say while Sarah watches on, swaying and twirling her hair around a finger, oblivious to any tension.

I look up at Oliver as he pulls me closer, nuzzling my neck, causing goosebumps to break out all over my body.

"I've known Lilly almost her whole life, and as soon as you let her go, I couldn't let the opportunity pass to snap her up and make her mine."

After this declaration, both Sarah and I stare at Oliver with identical looks of adoration, while Sebastian gives a dismissive sniff.

"Whatever, man. I'm just glad you both could make it this weekend." He turns to the group gathered nearby and yells, "Let's get this party started!" With this said, he throws his arm around Sarah, who is still shooting adoring looks at Oliver, and drags her off towards the "fun," leaving us to trail behind.

"What did I ever see in him?" I ask myself out loud.

"I don't know," answers Oliver, watching me, still holding me close. "That guy never deserved you."

At his response, my face heats with a happy flush, and I take a moment to bask in the glow of being Oliver's "girlfriend" before turning back to the task at hand. I have to get through the day (and the weekend) with my dignity and my heart intact.

CHAPTER 26

Lilly

WE MAKE OUR WAY OUT to the hotel lawn to where a delicious brunch spread had been laid out for all of us, and Oliver continues to hold my hand as we find a place to sit, by unspoken agreement as far away from the bridal couple as possible. As we introduce ourselves to the people around us, we find that Sarah's friends are an amiable group of people, and before too long, I've learned the backstory of everyone sitting with us, making fast friends.

As I chat with the lovely girl sitting next to me named Melanie, telling her all about Love, Lilly and the upcoming launch of my pop-up café, Oliver sits next to me, running his hand up and down my back, causing me to have delighted full-body shivers.

"You two are so cute," Melanie says, smiling as she notices me staring at Oliver. "How long have you been together?"

"Almost a year," I tell her, as practised.

"But we've been friends forever," Oliver chimes in. We are both following the script to perfection.

"And how did you move from friends to more?" Melanie asks with blatant curiosity, leaning her head on her hand and giving us her undivided attention.

"Well, I always wanted to be more than friends with Lilly, since we were teenagers, but unfortunately Lilly here was quick to put me firmly in the friend zone, and after that, it took me a while to convince her to let me out."

I stare at Oliver with wide eyes, forgetting that we're pretending, and say, "What?"

Oliver pokes me gently and gestures his head towards our audience.

"Oh, right? Yes, that's how it went," I fumble. "But can you blame me for keeping him at arm's length for so long? I mean, look at him!" I wave my hand in the general direction of his chest, arms, and abs. "The guy is a hottie. And back then, I thought there was no way any guy like that would want to be with me. My idea was that it was better to keep him in my life as a friend rather than risk losing him altogether." At this true-to-life confession, Oliver gives me a searching look, his eyes locking with mine.

"So what changed your mind?" Melanie asks, breaking the moment.

"He badgered me for months on end until I finally took pity on him and agreed to go on a date with him." I flash Oliver a cheeky grin.

Oliver pinches my side and throws in, "And I wooed her with so much charm that she couldn't resist me."

"That's so romantic," Melanie sighs. "I love a friends-to-lovers story." As I feel myself blush at this description, both with embarrassment and shame for lying to my new friends, I change the subject away from myself.

"So is anyone excited about a day of fun beach activities?" I ask with fake enthusiasm.

Melanie and a few of the girls nearby groan, with one saying, "What's so wrong with a day at the spa, anyway?"

I feel triumphant at this display of sister solidarity, and as I look at Oliver, I see that he's watching me with amusement and, from the corner of my eye, notice that Sebastian is getting up to address the group.

"Friends and family!" he yells, getting everyone's attention. "It's now time for us to get active!" In response to both cheers and boos, Sebastian puts his hands up and says, "It will be fun. Sarah and I are so looking forward to a day of games and competition. Aren't we, honey?" Sarah looks on, seeming a bit confused about what's taking place, and says nothing. To cover for the awkward silence left by his fiancée, Sebastian tells us about how they've set up teams for beach volleyball, which will then be followed by a game of tug of war, and the day will then finish with "friendly" touch football. It all sounds terrible to me, and from the faces around me, most of the guests seem to agree.

"Let's hope we're on the same team," Oliver says from beside me. "That way I can do the work for both of us, and you can just pretend to be taking part." I smile at him, thinking it's great that he can just read my mind, and then, dragging my feet, I get up to join in the festivities.

Three hours and many, many complaints from me later, the "fun" finally ends. As it turns out, both Sebastian and Oliver are competitive, and as each event rolled on, they became more intense with each other. Sebastian seemed to goad Oliver at every chance he got, trying to get a rise out of him, and Oliver, to his credit, did his best to focus his attention on me while also winning every game. I was just happy to stand at Oliver's side, saying random words of encouragement and watching him. Halfway through the beach volleyball match, his shirt came off, and I got the absolute pleasure of rubbing sunscreen all over his back. A favour that Oliver seemed all too happy to return. The aftermath of his warm skin under my hands, and then my warm skin under his, had me taking myself for a dip in the ocean to cool off.

And now we're back in the hotel room, having to get ready for the night ahead, the bachelor and bachelorette parties. The two groups will start off apart, with the girls having wine tasting and dinner beforehand and the guys playing some more sports-type activities, before the two groups will join back together at some beach bar nearby. Oliver has been taking everything in his stride, seeming to enjoy himself even while spending a weekend surrounded by strangers, something he has avoided doing in the past. Me? Well, I've loved every minute of our time together. Oliver has been playing the part of the doting boyfriend to perfection, holding my hand, caressing my arm, thigh, face at any chance, even giving me a few fleeting kisses on the cheek when the occasion called for it. Whoever ends up with Oliver will be a lucky girl because this guy is an amazing boyfriend.

I tell him this as we settle in our room later that day for a mandatory break from activities, sun kissed and covered in sand.

"Ollie, you should write a book on how to be a boyfriend, ten steps to being the best partner," I say as I flop down on the bed, exhausted by the sheer amount of physical activity I had to endure today.

"You're a pretty great girlfriend yourself," he replies, plopping down next to me and rolling on his side to face me. "We make a great team," he adds, gazing into my eyes, making my heart race.

I sit up, trying to get control of my runaway emotions. This is pretend, Lilly. You must not forget that.

"Are you sure you're OK going to this bro night tonight? It sounds painful, and you will have to spend time with Sebastian." Over the course of the day, both Oliver and I agreed that Sebastian is, in fact, the worst, and I can't imagine why Oliver would volunteer to spend additional time with him.

"It'll be fine. Just a couple of beers and some pool before I get to be with you," he replies, sending my heart racing some more. At this rate, I will have a full-blown heart attack before the weekend ends.

"OK, but feel free to leave at any time. I give you permission to ditch Sebastian and his gang of merry douche friends and come back to the room for some down time."

"I'm OK, Lil. Don't worry about me. Are you going to be OK spending the evening with Sarah? She's so weird," Oliver says with a puzzled smile. All day today, Sarah has been acting in a strange manner around me. I'm not sure if it's because I used to date Sebastian or if there's something just not quite right with her. It's been a stroke of luck that most of Sarah's friends are nice people who have made me feel accepted and welcome.

"I know, right? What's her problem? Do you think she's behaving strangely because she thinks I'm a threat to her relationship?"

Oliver raises an eyebrow, allowing his gaze to travel down my body and back up again, lingering on my face.

"Sometimes I wonder what you see when you look in the mirror, Lilly," he says at last. "Because one look at you is enough to cause any woman a lot of anxiety. You're gorgeous. And smart, funny, and kind. Sarah is bound to be jealous, and Sebastian is bound to regret having let you go."

I stare at Oliver as he's saying these wonderful things to me, my cheeks heating.

"You think I'm gorgeous?" I say in a hushed tone.

Oliver looks at me like I'm crazy. "Of course I think you're gorgeous, Lilly. I wish you could see the person I see when I look at you."

Unable to find an answer to this, finding myself speechless, I lie back down and face Oliver on the bed.

"I think you're gorgeous too," I finally say, a quiet confession.

Oliver smiles, the full-dimple smile, as we lie in bed just staring at each other, content to let this moment just be. Unfortunately, Amy, the queen of bad timing, chooses this exact moment to call me, her ringtone blasting through the room, breaking the mood. As I cross the room to answer the call and tell her to piss off, Oliver says he's going to use the shower and get ready for the evening.

"Lilly?" Amy yells as I answer the phone. "Where have you been? Why haven't you been returning my calls or texts or DMs? I'm dying to know what happened after the night in the one bed."

"Nothing happened," I say almost sadly. "Oliver was a perfect gentleman. He stayed on his side all night."

"Oh, boo, that's no fun," Amy says with a pout I can almost see through the phone.

"I did wake up wrapped around him like he was an enormous teddy bear I was hugging," I add, smiling at the image of our early-morning cuddle.

"You what?" she screeches, almost deafening me in one ear.

"It was nothing. I extricated myself before he woke up, and it's all been platonic ever since. For the most part."

"Spill," Amy demands.

"It's so confusing, Ames. We spent the day together, and it felt like we were really together, you know?"

"Ah, huh."

"But it's only pretend. Except it doesn't always feel like we're pretending. This was a big mistake, Ames. Now that I've had a taste of 'being with' Oliver, going back to being just friends is going to be impossible."

"Then make a move. What have you got to lose?"

"Everything. Too much," I tell her. "I love you guys too much to risk anything happening and then it blowing up in my face. And honestly, I think Oliver is just an excellent actor. No doubt he still sees me as Silly Lilly, the girl he has to rescue at an alarming frequency, and doesn't think of me romantically at all."

Before Amy can answer, Oliver exits the bathroom in just a towel, and I almost pass out.

"Amy, I have to go," I croak, my throat suddenly dry. "Call you later."

I hang up the phone and stare at Oliver, unable to do the polite thing and look away. Boy, this guy and his muscles. He should be in a museum somewhere.

"Sorry, Lilly. I left my clean clothes out here. Why don't you use the bathroom, and I can get dressed?"

This snaps me out of my Oliver-induced haze, and I nod with an audible gulp. I scurry around like a frightened mouse, avoiding Oliver's amused gaze, and sprint into the bathroom, slamming the door behind me. After that display, how am I going to survive another night in that bed alone with Oliver?

CHAPTER 27

Lilly

AFTER ANOTHER LONG, COLD SHOWER to get my mind out of the gutter, I spend some time getting ready for the evening ahead. I coax my hair out of its usual frizz and into some sexy beach waves. I take extra care with my make-up, attempting a smoky eye and adding a slick of pink lip gloss, and dress in a short, flirty tropical-print summer dress, with a skirt that flares when I spin around. After adding a pair of high-heeled sandals to complete the look, I exit the bathroom in a cloud of perfume. Oliver looks away from the TV show he's watching as I enter the room and just stares. Not saying anything, he stands and walks almost unwittingly towards me, stopping mere inches from me, and says finally, "You are beautiful."

I blush hard from head to toe and do a small curtsy. "Thank you, kind sir. You don't look so bad yourself." Oliver reaches out to tuck a stray hair behind my ear, stroking my cheek, almost like he can't help himself.

"Are you sure you want to go out tonight?" he asks out of nowhere, his voice taking on a husky quality. "Maybe we can stay in again."

Tempted, oh so tempted, I say with reluctance, "I've committed to going tonight, Ol. And I'm actually looking forward to hanging out with the girls. And I didn't spend all this time getting ready to stay in the room all night," I add with a smile.

Oliver waits a beat and then nods. "OK, then we'd better get going."

Given we've spent all day glued to each other's side, I'm reluctant to part ways with Oliver, holding on to his hand in the elevator down to the reception, where each of the parties are meeting for the evening, not letting go until I literally have to.

"Have fun, Lilly. And be careful. I'll see you soon," Oliver says as he follows the boys out of the foyer, looking back at me one last time over his shoulder before he rounds the corner and is out of sight.

"Your boyfriend is so mad about you," Melanie says from my side, with a wistful sigh. "He watches you, always checking to see if you're OK. He adores you."

I turn to look at Melanie, my mind filled with doubt as to what she's seeing. "Really?"

Melanie gives me a strange look and adds, "Yes, he's so protective of you. Every time another guy got even a little bit close to you, there he was, by your side, staking his claim."

Huh. I think back on the day. Oliver did seem possessive. Like during one of the downtimes we had, between beach volleyball and tug of war earlier today, when I was talking to one of Sebastian's friends, Oliver appeared out of nowhere, grabbing me around the waist and kissing my temple. Could it be he was jealous? Or is he just very good at acting the part of a protective boyfriend?

"That's just the way Oliver is," I tell Melanie. "He has always looked out for me."

"Well, you're a lucky girl. He's delicious."

I agree with Melanie's description, while also feeling a bit of possessiveness of my own, and turn to see Sarah gathering the group together to head off for the wine tasting and dinner portion of the night.

Ninety minutes and many wines later, I'm in my happy place, feeling relaxed and free. The wine tasting was a lot of fun. Sarah's friends included me in all their girl talk, and after we finished dinner, we walked over to the local beach bar to continue the night with more drinks and some dancing.

After we arrive at the bar, Sarah orders us a round of shots and then some more shots, and before too long, I'm thinking it's a grand idea to get up on the bar to dance. I grab the hand of my new best friend Melanie and drag her up with me as some pop tune blares from the jukebox. As I break into an impromptu line dance, I look up to see Oliver leaning against a wall, watching me from across the room, a small smile on his lips. His beautiful lips. I wave to him and manoeuvre my way down off the bar. Oliver makes quick work of getting to me to make sure I don't fall, and we end up on the dance floor together at the same time.

"Ollie! You're here!" I give him an unsteady hug.

"You look like you're having fun," he replies, shielding me from the people dancing around us.

"Did you have fun with Seb the douche?" I ask in a whisper shout.

Oliver laughs and shakes his head, looking around to make sure I have offended no one. "I had fun but clearly not as much fun as you."

"There has been wine," I say. "And tequila. And more tequila. I'm feeling good." I raise my hand for a high five, wobbling a bit on my heels.

After giving me a half-hearted high five in return, Oliver smiles at me and says, "Stay here while I get you some water. OK, Lil? Don't go anywhere."

"Yes, sir!" I mock salute him, swaying to the music.

Oliver disappears to the bar, and I look around. This has been a wonderful night, I think to myself in a happy, drunken state. The music is great, and Oliver is here with me. What more could I ask for? As I'm thinking this, I feel a pair of hands on my hips and turn around, expecting Oliver, only to be greeted by some random guy asking me to dance instead. Hmm, he seems nice. There's no harm if I dance with him while I wait for Oliver to return. I smile at him and nod, and we move clumsily together to the music—this guy is cute. In another world, one where Oliver doesn't exist, I may have been interested in him.

In a sudden movement, Oliver appears behind my dance partner, looking at me, asking me with his eyes for permission to cut in. I give him a little nod, and he takes no time, grabbing my waist, hurrying us away from the cute guy, while pulling me closer to him at the same time. I wave an apology to the stranger as he backs away and let myself relax against Oliver, moving to the music with him. As he pulls me even closer, Oliver tucks me in under his chin and lets out a sigh. I nuzzle in, feeling secure, and I think to myself, This is where I belong.

Oliver continues to sway us from side to side, pressing his lips to the top of my head.

I lean back ever so slightly and peer up at him. "I'm going to kiss you." Oliver stops moving, his eyes flaring as he gives me an intense look, and I add, "As soon as I figure out why there are two of you." With terrible coordination, I attempt to cover one eye and then the other to make the two versions of Oliver merge back into one, and Oliver puts his arm around my waist, guiding me off the dance floor. Feeling dizzy now, I lean into him, full of regret that our moment has passed but also struggling to stand upright.

"Do you think you will make the walk back to the hotel room?" Oliver asks, looking concerned.

"Yup," I say, popping the p. "Let's just wait for the room to stop spinning first." As I look around, a little dazed, Oliver grabs a bottle of water for me from the bar and encourages me to take a sip. When I feel somewhat better, Oliver pulls me close again, his arm banded around my back, half guiding, half carrying me towards the door.

"Bye, friends!" I yell to no one in particular as we walk out.

Oliver lets out a small chuckle, shaking his head at me.

"I'm sorry, Ollie," I tell him in a small voice once we're outside, feeling bad that he's forced to take care of me again.

"It's OK, Lil. I'm glad you had a good night. And I love taking care of you."

I walk in a zigzag pattern, unable to maintain a straight line, and as such, it takes longer than necessary to get back to the hotel, by which time the tequila high has worn off and things have taken a turn for the worse.

"I don't feel so good," I groan as we approach our room. Oliver takes one look at me and hurries us inside. We make a dash for the bathroom, where I throw up all the tequila and wine and everything I ever consumed in my entire life. And then I throw up some more. When I finally feel well enough to sit back, Oliver crouches next to me, patting my face with a wet cloth, asking if I have finished.

I nod and say in a low voice, "Oh god, I wish you hadn't seen that," knowing I'm going to be mortified by this forever.

Oliver shushes me, picking me up and carrying me to the bed. After laying me down, he makes quick work of removing my shoes and tucking the blanket around me.

"Do you think you will be OK now?" he asks.

I groan, vowing, not for the first time, to never drink again, and say weakly, "I think so." As I bury my head in my pillow, I pray for the sweet relief of unconsciousness to get me out of the situation. I open one eye and see Oliver is lying down next to me, watching me with a worried frown on his face.

"I've left some water next to the bed for you. Wake me up if you feel sick again."

"OK, Ol," I mumble. I love you, I think to myself as I slip into blissful oblivion.

CHAPTER 28

Oliver

S HE LOVES ME? IS THAT what Lilly just mumbled before she fell asleep? She loves me? As I lie back and watch Lilly sleep, she looks so peaceful now, so different from the girl I saw attempting to line dance on top of a bar. I smile to myself at the mental picture of Lilly dancing on the bar, her face lighting up when she caught sight of me. Could this mean she has feelings for me too? It has been a weekend filled with moments of togetherness. Could it all be real? Or is Lilly that good of an actress?

I think back to this morning and stifle a groan at the thought of waking up with Lilly in my arms, wrapped around me like a little boa constrictor. She was as warm and soft as I knew she would be, and I savoured every minute, keeping as still as possible to drag the moment out. And when I felt her wake up and attempt to move away, I couldn't resist pulling her back in for a little longer. I know I was being a coward by pretending to be asleep (so much pretending this weekend) and feigning ignorance of our morning snuggle when Lilly catapulted herself out of bed. It just seemed that that was how Lilly wanted to play it, and what Lilly wants, Lilly gets.

After spending today with her, playing the role of her boy-friend, I know now, without a doubt, that Lilly is the person I should be with. When I compare it with the time I spent with Emma, well, there's no real comparison to be made. With Lilly, I can't stop myself from touching her. I have to be near her all the time. I'm possessive and jealous, emotions I've never experienced before. And above all else, I'm happy. So happy. And it has all happened under the guise of helping her out. At this thought, I let out a small chuckle, as I marvel at the idea that Lilly is grateful for my help this weekend. That she thinks I'm doing her a favour. Lilly has no idea just how many times I've wished this relationship were real.

I look over at Lilly's sleeping form and take her hand in mine, settling back to get some sleep. Big day tomorrow. It may just be the day when Lilly and I finally stop pretending.

CHAPTER 29

Lilly

I WAKE UP THE NEXT morning with a jackhammer pounding in my head and roll over gingerly to see Oliver asleep next to me. As I glance down, I see he's holding my hand. Sigh. I wish I did not feel like someone ran me over with a truck, a truck full of tequila no less, so I could enjoy this moment, but instead, I need to find a way to make this pounding in my brain stop. With reluctance, I let go of Oliver's hand and sit up. Once the room stops spinning, I see that a glass of water and a bottle of Advil have been left next to the bed. So typical of Oliver, always so thoughtful. With shaking hands, I swallow two tablets and drain the glass. I stand up, swaying as I do so. How much did I drink last night? I try to remember the details of the evening, recalling the wine tasting and the bar. There was tequila. I can still taste that—and did I dance on the bar top? Flashes of images play in my mind as I make my way to the bathroom, each step causing a sharp pain in my temple. I see myself dancing—yes, indeed, that was on the bar top—then with some random guy and then with Oliver. A glimpse of me wobbling out of the door, and then, oh no, Oliver saw me throw up. Why, Lilly?

Why must you do this to yourself? There's no way he can see me as a sexy grown-up potential life partner when I keep getting myself into these situations.

I notice the time and wake Oliver up from across the room, letting him know we have an hour before the wedding begins, then get started on the task of making myself look human again. I take a shower to wash off the stench of alcohol before drying my hair into soft waves, then spend some time on my make-up, trying to cover the damages of a night of partying followed by a horrendous hangover. Once I'm happy that I look as good as I'm going to get, I wrap a large towel around myself and leave the bathroom. As I enter the bedroom, Oliver is sitting up in bed, scrolling through his phone.

"Bathroom is free," I tell him as his head shoots up to look at me. Oliver scans me up and down, lingering on the places where the towel ends, and he edges his way out of the bed.

"Sorry again about last night," I tell him as he gathers up what he needs to get ready.

He looks at me and smiles his dimple smile. "Lil, you were fine. You had a fun night. You're allowed to let your hair down now and then. And you're an adorable drunk person."

I blush and smile back at him, nodding in gratitude. "Well, thanks for looking after me."

"My pleasure," he says, his eyes still on me as he leaves the room.

Once alone, I pull out the Perfect Dress from where it's hanging in the closet and slip it on. As I look at myself in the mirror, I let out a sigh. It's just as beautiful as I remember. The dress is a soft champagne colour, with red, pink, and purple flowers embroidered on the bust. It has thin spaghetti straps, it fits snug to the waist, and from there, it flows to the ground. And the best part is the back, which is bare with only soft criss-crossing straps holding it together, stopping just above my tail bone. It's the most stunning gown I've ever worn, and with my hair styled with soft curls done in an elaborate half up do, and nude heels, the outfit is complete. As I wait, filled with nervous energy, for Oliver to come out of the bathroom, I add a few things to my evening bag and fiddle with my jewellery. When the door opens and he steps out into the bedroom, I hold my breath, waiting for him to get his first look at me.

Oliver stops short and stares. He looks me up and down and swallows hard.

"You're perfect, Lilly," he says finally, his voice gruff with emotion.

"You like?" I ask, turning around to show him the back.

"Very much," he says, his voice still strained. "I think it's safe to say that no one will look at the bride with you there looking like that."

I smile at him, knowing he's saying this to make me feel good, understanding the assignment of the revenge dress, and I finally take a moment to properly look at him. Wow! Oliver in a black dress suit is drool worthy.

"You look drool worthy," I say to him and then give myself a mental slap in the face.

Oliver throws his head back and laughs.

"Did I say that out loud?" I ask, blushing with embarrassment.

"That's OK, Lil. I'm happy you think of me that way."

Oliver steps towards me and tucks my hair behind my ear while I pick an imaginary piece of lint off his jacket. Any excuse to touch him.

"You ready to go?" he asks, offering me his arm.

"Lead the way," I say, full of excitement for the day ahead. Terrible hangover all but forgotten.

We arrive at the small chapel located on the grounds of the hotel, and Oliver puts his arm protectively around my back, his thumb stroking small circles on my bare skin while we wait to be seated.

"Are you with the bride or groom?" an adorable little girl with a lisp asks us, obviously taking on the role of usher.

"We're with the groom, I guess?" I tell her.

As we follow her to our seats, Oliver keeps his arm in place around me, and as we sit down, I use this opportunity to snuggle in close to him. I look up and see Oliver staring down at me with a smile, and I sigh, filled with happiness.

I move my attention to the front of the chapel, where Sebastian is waiting with his groomsmen and the priest, fiddling with his bow tie, looking nervous. With some time to spare, I give him an objective once over, still unable to figure out what I ever saw in him, and Amy's words come back to haunt me: "You tend to go for guys that are nothing like Oliver." It's so true; Sebastian is shallow and materialistic. Fickle and vain. I'm so glad he dumped me all those months ago, bringing me to this very moment here with Oliver.

As the music starts, we all turn as Sarah enters the chapel and makes the slow walk down the aisle. She looks beautiful. Even though her behaviour has been strange this weekend, I have to admit that the bride looks stunning, and watching the look in her eyes as she makes her way towards Sebastian, my eyes fill with tears. Oliver, noticing this, squeezes my hand and pulls me in closer. And we stay like this throughout the whole ceremony as we watch Sebastian, my ex-boyfriend, and Sarah become man and wife.

Once the formalities of the ceremony are over, we make our way to the cocktail hour. I grab a glass of water, shying away from any and all alcohol, and pull Oliver over with me to talk to Melanie.

"Hey, Lilly!" She smiles when she sees me. "How are you feeling after last night?"

"Ugh, trying not to think too much about last night, Mel," I tell her. "I can't believe how much I had to drink."

"You weren't the only one," Melanie whispers to me. "Sarah was up most of the night throwing up!"

"No!" I gasp in horror. What a terrible way to spend the night before your wedding day.

"Yes," Melanie confirms. "She pulled it together for the big day though."

We both turn to look at where Sarah is greeting the guests, seeming no worse for wear from the antics of last night.

"You were lucky to have this gorgeous man to take care of you," Melanie continues, causing Oliver to blush while giving us a small bow.

"Yes, I've been lucky a lot throughout my life to have this gorgeous man taking care of me," I tell her, gazing into Oliver's deep-brown eyes with gratitude.

Oliver holds my gaze, saying nothing, while Melanie clears her throat and makes an excuse to leave us alone.

"Would you like to dance, Lilly?" Oliver asks when the music plays. As I hear that the first song up is an acoustic version of "Perfect" by Ed Sheeran, I nod in agreement.

As I stand in Oliver's arms, swaying to a song about friends who become lovers, I think this may be a perfect moment. And it's so much better to dance with Oliver when I'm sober.

"What are you thinking?" Oliver whispers into my ear, sending all those delicious shivers down my spine again. This is a feeling I could get used to.

"Just how nice it is to dance with you without being intoxicated," I tell him. "It's nice to be in your arms without the room spinning as well."

I lift my head from where it has been resting on Oliver's chest and take a moment to just stare at him. At his dark-brown eyes and his plump lips and—

Then Oliver's lips are on mine, and it is perfect. It's our first kiss, and it's just as I imagined it would be. Oliver's lips are soft but insistent, kissing me almost hungrily, and I match his intensity, putting everything I feel for him into it. As the kiss deepens, Oliver runs his hands through my hair, ruining my well-put-together do while I grab the front of his shirt, trying to pull him even closer. We kiss for hours and only seconds, and before I want it to end, Oliver, with obvious reluctance, lifts his head.

"You have no idea how long I've wanted to do that," he tells me, his voice thick with emotion.

I stand still in his arms, a little shocked by this admission, and then pull his lips back down to mine. I'm not ready for this to be over.

This second kiss is deeper and more passionate than the first. Oliver pulls me even closer to him, our bodies crushed up against each other, as we devour each other's mouths. When I go to pull away to catch my breath, Oliver's lips follow mine, as if he's unwilling or unable to break the contact. It's the most earth-shattering kiss I've ever had, and I can't imagine going back to kissing anyone other than Oliver again.

When the song ends and our surroundings come back into focus, Oliver slowly pulls away, both of us breathing hard from what has just occurred.

"Was that OK, Lilly?" Oliver asks once he has his breath back.

"Hmmmm," I reply, still unable to form a coherent thought. Oliver and I just kissed! And it was magical and perfect. And what happens now?

"What happens now?" I blurt out.

Oliver, having regained control of himself a lot faster than me, smiles and says, "Now we get you some food and maybe have another dance again after?"

I look around to see that lunch has been served, and we're expected to take a seat. I hold on tight to Oliver's offered hand, and I walk with him on shaky legs to the buffet table before serving myself some lunch that I know I have no intention of eating. All the while trying to figure out what just happened and what it will all mean when the weekend ends.

CHAPTER 30

Lilly

A s THE WEDDING FESTIVITIES CONTINUE, I watch it all through a fog. Oliver and I kissed. And now he's holding my hand, stroking my leg, and keeping me close, and I can't figure out what is real and what is pretend. The lines are all blurred. We need to talk about what has happened, but with people around and my new friends vying for my attention—why must I make friends wherever I go?—it's difficult to get some time alone. Oliver, for his part, seems unaffected by what has occurred. Chatting to the people around us, oblivious to my inner turmoil. Did it not mean as much to him as it did to me? He said it was something he had wanted to do, so it must have some meaning, but why wasn't he shaken to the core like I was?

Oliver, perhaps sensing my inner conflict, picks up my hand that he's holding and brushes his lips over it. He pulls me up from where I'm seated and, turning to the group at our table, says, "I think I need some alone time with my beautiful Lilly here." The women all sigh at this and give me a wistful look as Oliver pulls me back onto the dance floor, otherwise known as the scene of the crime.

"Lilly, are you OK? You've been uncharacteristically quiet throughout lunch," Oliver says as we begin another slow dance together.

"I'm a bit confused," I tell him, deciding to be honest.

"About what?"

"Are we still pretending?" I whisper, needing to know he's feeling what I'm feeling.

Oliver stares at me for several moments while my heartbeat takes off some more.

"Lilly, none of this has been pretending for me."

As I take a second to digest what this means—none of what? None of the kiss? The weekend? Sarah gets on the microphone to announce that she will throw the bouquet and that all the single ladies should gather in the middle of the dance floor. Melanie, being my new best friend, grabs me out of Oliver's arms and pulls me into the middle of the pack.

"We've got this!" Melanie says, looking serious. Feeling nervous, I look around and see some of the ladies standing next to us doing hamstring stretches. This appears to be a serious sport for some.

"I don't think Sarah would want me to have her bouquet," I tell Melanie, trying to edge my way out of the bunch of hungry-looking single women.

"Nonsense," Melanie admonishes me. "See that yummy man you have back there?" she says as my gaze follows hers to where Oliver is standing watching me. "This may be the signal he needs to pop the question."

"Oh no," I tell her, attempting to backtrack out of this conversation. "We aren't there yet."

"You may not be, but that man over there is so hopelessly in love with you. I'm surprised he hasn't proposed to you yet."

My face warms at this, and I turn to look at Oliver again. Could Melanie and Amy be right? Could Oliver have feelings for me? As I stand pondering this thought, I'm suddenly crushed under the weight of four women, all fighting to catch the bouquet, which I only just saw was thrown directly at me.

Once the lucky lady—is that Melanie?—has the bouquet in her proud possession, I'm given enough room to pick myself up from the floor. As I stand, Oliver is making his way to me with a worried frown on his face.

"Lilly, are you OK? You got absolutely smashed by the crowd."

I inspect myself for injuries, ensuring that the Perfect Dress is unharmed, and I see a small cut on my elbow. I show it to Oliver with a pitiful whimper. "Do you think I will survive?"

Oliver lets out a relieved breath, giving my elbow a soft kiss, and smiles. "Those women were ruthless. I didn't think you'd make it out of there alive."

"Never underestimate the power of a bouquet and a room full of women wanting to be the next to get married," I say as I limp off the dance floor.

We sit back down at our table as I get my breath back, and I see that the wedding is starting the wrap up. With the formalities all complete, the bride and groom having said their goodbyes, it's now time to get some cake and start the long ride home. I look at Oliver, feeling a wave of sadness wash over me, knowing our weekend of pretend is over. But amid it all, I now have some hope. Maybe it doesn't have to be pretend moving forward?

"OK, walking wounded," Oliver says to me, holding my hand and pulling me up to stand. "I think it's time to go."

"Cake first," I insist.

"Of course," he replies, leading the way to the cake table. He picks up two plates of two different cake flavours—so I can try both—and we make our way back to our hotel room. Once there, I polish off the cake, then step into the bathroom to take off my Perfect Dress and return to my normal, boring clothes.

While I'm doing this, I hear Oliver packing up his belongings, and before too long, we're ready to go. As I turn towards the door, Oliver touches my elbow, stopping me in my tracks. He gives me another one of his intense looks before saying, "We should probably talk about the kiss?"

Finally, an acknowledgment.

"What kiss?" I pretend to think about it. "We kissed?"

Oliver smiles at me and roughly pulls me closer.

"You don't remember?" he says, his lips inches from mine.

"Hmm, I may need my memory refreshed."

Before I can even finish my sentence, Oliver has crushed his lips to mine, and it's better than the other kisses. This one is hot and almost brutal and goes on and on until we force ourselves apart, breathless and aroused.

"That kiss," he says in a low voice, a voice that is doing things to my insides.

"Yup. That was a kiss," I reply, still shell shocked by the power of it.

"So we should talk about it?"

"Yes, definitely, we should talk about it," I say as I pull his mouth back to mine, now addicted to kissing him. This kiss is soft and tender, and I melt into it, feeling it down to my toes.

"We should go," Oliver says after a long moment, lifting his head from mine, gently rubbing his nose against mine as he does so, his eyes filled with longing. "We have to check out, like two minutes ago," he adds, looking at his watch.

Still in a daze, I nod and allow him to usher me out of the room and down the elevator. I let him take care of the paperwork as I float around the reception area. When I see Melanie, I promise to keep in touch and give her a hug.

"I'll come and visit your pop-up café, Lilly," she tells me, her voice raised with excitement. "I follow you on Instagram now, so I will stay up to date with all your developments."

"That's great, Mel. I hope we get to meet up again soon," I tell her with full sincerity.

"Absolutely," she replies, looking at where Oliver is making his way over to me. "And who knows? Maybe yours will be the next wedding I'm invited to." And with that little bombshell, she gives me another hug and waves goodbye to Oliver as she races out the front door.

"You ready to go, Lil?" Oliver asks, taking my hand in his like it's the most natural thing for him to do.

I look at him and then at our joined hands and take a deep breath. "Yep, you lead, and I will follow."

CHAPTER 31

Lilly

A s I settle into Oliver's car, I have a mental conversation as to ways of bringing up the topic of the kisses and what it could all mean. It should be a straightforward conversation: "Oliver, we kissed. I love you. Can we get married now?" However, it's proving to be difficult to broach. What if Oliver was just swept up in the moment? What if he intends for us to return to just friends now that the weekend is over? With so many what ifs swirling around my head, I'm paralysed into saying nothing. Hoping Oliver will take the lead, I sit in silence, staring out of the window, watching the world go by.

A few minutes into the drive, Oliver leans over and takes my hand. He holds it in his, resting both our hands on my thigh as he continues to watch the road ahead. I smile at this gesture, thinking this is Oliver's way of letting me know that the pretend portion of the weekend has finished and he's still in this with me, and I relax into my seat. Maybe we aren't ready for the important conversation yet, but sometimes actions speak louder than words.

At some point, I must fall asleep, because before I know it, we're approaching Oliver's house. As I wake up, I feel a bit confused, wondering why Oliver has driven us here and not to my apartment, and I look at him with raised eyebrows.

"I'm not ready for the weekend to end yet," he tells me simply. "I thought maybe you'd want to spend the evening with me. We can get some dinner and talk?" Oliver looks a little unsure of himself, and my heart squeezes at his display of vulnerability.

"That sounds perfect," I tell him. "I'm not ready for this weekend to be over either."

Oliver grins at me and focuses back on the road, taking the last few turns to get us home. As we approach the driveway, I have butterflies in my stomach, equal parts thrilled and nervous at the thought of the evening ahead. Maybe Oliver and I can sort out our relationship status now, once and for all. Oliver parks the car in the garage and gets out, rounding the car to open my door. I take his offered hand and step out of the car, my whole body warmed by his display of public affection. As we walk towards the front door, a familiar figure is pacing up and down the porch area. Emma. No, this can't be. What's she doing here?

As she hears us approach, her head jerks towards us, her gaze zeroing in on our joined hands. Oliver, looking at Emma and then me, drops my hand and steps towards her.

"Emma? What are you doing here?" he asks in a strained voice.

"We need to talk. In private," Emma adds, looking at me.

As I stare at Oliver, willing him to tell her to go and ask me to stay, I'm blindsided when he hesitates and looks at me. Is he really going to leave me and go to her? After everything we experienced together this weekend? The thought of Oliver going back to the perfect Emma causes a sharp pain in my chest. I reach up to absently rub it as I silently will him to not do this. I need him to use this opportunity to make me feel like I'm the one for him.

I watch in disbelief as Oliver takes two steps away from me towards Emma, and I know the choice has been made. He's going back to the girl I know he's supposed to be with, and I will go back to being the girl he could never love that way. The pain in my chest builds as I take a step away from him, looking in my bag for my phone, now desperate to call an Uber or a friend or anyone to get me out of here. I finally find my phone, and I have ten missed calls from Amy, as well as a dozen text messages, all warning me that Emma is waiting and telling me to not return home. Too late now, Amy, I think to myself. As this is going on, I see out the corner of my eye that Oliver has inched closer to Emma, moving the two of them away from me, further cementing in my mind that his choice is made. Am I overreacting? Possibly, but after the kisses we just shared, my heart is too vulnerable to deal with any sort of rejection. Even more desperate now to get away, I call Amy and tell her to come outside and rescue me.

"You're outside?" Amy yells into the phone in place of the traditional hello.

"Yes, come and get me out of here," I whisper, pleading with her.

In no time at all, hurricane Amy is rushing out of the house, shooting Emma and Oliver a dirty look as she runs past them. As she reaches me, she gives me a side hug, muttering under her breath, "What on earth happened here?"

"I can't get into it now," I tell her, trying to convey a sense of urgency with my voice. "Please get me out of here." I feel the sting of tears in my eyes and try to hold myself together. Oliver and Emma don't get to see me fall apart.

I look up to see Oliver looking at me with a pained expression, all flustered and confused, yet he still doesn't make a move towards me to stop me from leaving. Unable to continue to watch what is happening in front of my eyes, in a sharp motion, I turn away from him and follow Amy to her car.

Amy, being less tactful than me, turns to Oliver and says, a warning in her tone, "We'll talk about this later."

After I get into Amy's car, I sink into the seat and can't look at Oliver as tears begin to fall. Amy shoots me a worried look and speeds out of the driveway. I turn to look back one more time, and Oliver is watching us drive away before he walks back towards Emma. After seeing this, I feel what little is left of my control slip away, and I start to sob. Amy, who is driving like a Formula One driver on race day in her attempt to hasten my escape, looks at me again and curses Oliver under her breath.

"What happened this weekend, Lil?" she asks at last, breaking the silence.

As I think back on how perfect the weekend was, hangover and all, I cry harder. How could I have been so stupid to think that Oliver has genuine feelings for me? He's clearly still in love with his ex-girlfriend, the perfect Emma, and I'm just foolish enough to get caught up in the fantasy of it all.

"I'll tell you when we get to my place," I say through my tears. "I need wine and cupcakes to get through this story."

Amy nods, her face filled with sympathy. "Whatever has happened, Lil, we can fix it."

I shake my head at Amy and think to myself, There's no fixing this.

Once we arrive at my apartment and have both snuggled into the comfort of my couch, I pull a blanket up to my chin and attempt to stop crying. Amy, looking worried, has poured some wine, grabbed some tissues, and put a plate of cupcakes in front of us.

"Are you ready to tell me what happened?" Amy asks.

I look at Amy through blurry eyes and tell her about the weekend, all the details, leaving out nothing. From sharing a bed, to the PDAs, to the drunken bachelorette party, all the way through to the dance floor kiss.

"You kissed?" she squeals, caught up in the excitement.

"We kissed," I confirm with a half smile. "And it was perfect. The most mind-blowing kiss of my life. And then we kissed some more."

"So how did you go from mind-blowing kisses to crying on your couch?"

"It was all going so well. We were moving towards something. Oliver drove us back to your place to spend the evening together and talk, and I thought we were on the same page. And then we get to your house, and..." I trail off.

"Emma," Amy fills in the rest.

"Emma," I repeat. "As soon as he saw her, he dropped my hand like it was burning him. He couldn't get away from me fast enough."

"What do you mean?" Amy asks.

"He moved away from me, towards her. Like he was trying to cover for the fact that we were holding hands. Like he didn't want her to see us together. And in that moment, I just knew..." I trail off again.

"What, what did you know?"

"That he's not over her. That what we had this weekend isn't real. That I'm not good enough for him," I tell her, tears now streaming down my face.

Amy looks at me, tears filling her eyes as well.

"I'm sorry he did that to you, and that it made you feel that way," she starts. "But have you given any thought to the idea that maybe things aren't exactly as they seem?"

"It all seemed pretty clear to me," I say, feeling so miserable.

Amy looks at me and takes my hand. "Lilly, you know I love you, and when it comes to this, I'm always on your side?" I nod, encouraging her to continue. "But I think a lot of the way you have reacted to this situation is coming from your own insecurities." As I wince at this, I look away from Amy, thinking about what she's saying.

"Let's look at the situation: Oliver spent the whole weekend all over you. You shared several very hot kisses." I blush as she says this. "And then you have an awkward moment when you get home, where Oliver does not react exactly the way you would want him to. And now you think you never had a chance with him. That you aren't worthy. Lilly, that's not a healthy way to approach a relationship," she finishes, taking a gulp of her wine.

After staring at Amy for a long while, pondering what she has said, I'm not sure I can agree with her. I saw the way Oliver looked at Emma. He looked like he needed to get to her to what? Reassure her he wasn't with me? That they still had a chance to be together? And then the way he dropped my hand and left me to go to her. I just can't move past the rejection of it all. I tell this to Amy, who nods in agreement.

"You don't have to get over this right now. Just promise me you will think about what I've said. That when emotions aren't running so high, you will give Oliver a chance to tell his side of the story. And that you will look deeper into why someone as amazing as you seems to think you're not good enough."

"OK, Ames. I'll think about it, but it's hard not to think the problem is me when it keeps happening to me. And why would someone as amazing as Oliver want to be with me when he can be with the super successful, super polished Emma? Even my own parents don't think I'm anything special."

At this, Amy pulls me into a big hug. "Lilly, that is absolutely not true. Your parents just don't understand you; it doesn't mean they don't love you."

I stare at the face of my best friend, knowing she sees me in a way most people do not, and attempt a small smile.

"It's true," Amy continues. "You need to speak to your parents, let them know they make you feel this way."

"I don't think I can," I say, thinking about how terrible that conversation would be. How non-receptive my parents would be to my thoughts on the matter. "I've always been a disappointment to them. See how they love talking to you about work? They understand you. You speak the same language. You're the daughter they wish I could be."

Amy watches me, her eyes sad, not having a response to this, while I have another cupcake and feel even more sorry for myself. Now I'm feeling unloved by both Oliver and my parents. Terrible day to be me.

"Do you want me to stay here with you tonight?" Amy asks, changing the subject. "I don't fancy going home and seeing either Oliver or Emma right now, anyway."

As I think about the fact that Oliver and Emma may be together right now, the dried-up tears start again, and I sink lower into the couch.

"Yes, please. And let's not talk about men, or parents, or anything else of substance. Let's find a show on Netflix and binge until I fall asleep."

"Deal. You pick a show, and I'll get some reinforcements," Amy says, going into the kitchen to get more snacks.

I pick up my phone, turning it on silent so I'm not tempted to listen out for calls or texts from Oliver, and turn on the new season of Top Chef. As Amy sits down next to me, I give her a small, gratitude-filled hug and settle in for an evening of mind-numbing reality TV goodness. And attempt to not think about Oliver for the rest of the night.

CHAPTER 32

Oliver

I watch Lilly leave with a sinking feeling in my stomach and turn towards Emma.

"What are you doing here?" I ask her, knowing my tone is harsh but not able to find it in me to care.

"I came to give you another chance. But clearly you don't want a chance with me. Despite how long we were together, you took no time to get over me. Are you in love with her?" she asks, her words demanding but her voice shaking with emotion.

I sigh as I walk away from Emma to unpack the car and give myself some room to breathe. If I don't, I will snap at her again, and she doesn't deserve that after all we've been through together.

Emma follows me. "Just tell me. I'm right, aren't I? As soon as we broke up, you went to her?"

I know I owe her the truth. So I turn to look at her, the "perfect" woman, according to Lilly, and I feel nothing.

"Yes," I tell her. "I went to her hoping she would finally give me a chance."

At this, Emma's face turns sad, her eyes filling with tears. "Then why did you leave her just now and come to me? Why didn't you just tell me to go?" she asks, sounding confused.

I can't understand my reaction to the situation myself. It's not like I have any lingering feelings for Emma. I know I don't want to get back together with her. Am I so used to being the good guy that I put the needs of Emma ahead of Lilly? Or am I subconsciously sabotaging things with Lilly before they even begin? Everything this weekend with Lilly has been so perfect. Am I too scared to actually be with her, for fear of things going wrong?

None of this makes any sense, and I hate feeling this out of control. All I know is that I just made a decision, a split-second decision, and it may be one that haunts me for some time.

"I didn't want to hurt you further by flaunting it in front of you," I tell her with brutal honesty. "And I didn't want to give you the chance to say something hurtful to Lilly. You haven't been very kind to her, and she doesn't deserve the hate you send her way."

Emma has the decency to blush at this. "So that's it? You two are together now?"

"I thought we were getting there." I look in the direction of Amy's long-gone car. "Now I'm not so sure. I may have blown it before it even began."

Emma is quiet for a moment, thinking about what I just said, and maybe she sees something in my face that tells her what my words cannot, but to my surprise, she takes a deep breath and brushes my arm in sympathy.

"You really love her, don't you?"

I nod, grateful that she's giving me a chance to explain what's going on with Lilly and me, and before I can stop myself, I'm telling her everything that I've kept hidden for so long.

"I've always had strong feelings for Lilly, ever since we were kids growing up together. I never thought we could work though. So she has kind of existed as an unattainable fantasy for me. She's the person people gravitate towards, the one who has all the fun and creates all the mess, and I'm just the person that cleans up that mess. Who wants to be with that person?"

Emma gives me a small smile and puts her hand up, and I wince at my thoughtless words.

"I don't mean anything by that," I hasten to reassure her. "And when you and I were together, I wasn't thinking about Lilly. You have to believe that."

Emma nods with understanding, and I continue, my thoughts back on Lilly.

"I just never thought she would want to be with someone like me. She put me firmly in the friend zone for all these years, and it worked for us. And if I'm being honest, the feelings she inspires in me, they scare me sometimes. I feel out of control, and out of my depth, and..." I trail off, lost in my thoughts.

"And you wanted to avoid that by being with someone who doesn't inspire such big emotions?"

Again, I wince at how harsh my words are, knowing I'm not painting my relationship with Emma in the best light.

"I wanted to be with someone similar to me," I say instead, trying to convey to her that I really thought we were well suited. "You're so polished, and smart, and organised."

"Oliver, what you're describing are the traits you should want in a secretary, not a partner," Emma says, still taking everything I'm telling her with grace. Reverting back to the Emma I knew when we first got together, the Emma that wasn't so quick to snap at people.

"I know that now. I know now that all the things I thought were important in a partner, well, they really aren't. It's how they make you feel that's important. What I want is someone who brings colour into my life. Someone who makes me laugh, and loosens me up. I want Lilly," I finish, feeling more miserable as the minutes go by.

"Well, it sounds like you've finally figured out who you should be with. And even though you may have blown it a little bit tonight by not telling me to piss off and sweeping her off her feet into the house, I'm sure you will be able to fix it."

She then gives me a small hug, surprising me further, and whispers, "You need to go to her, and you need to fight for her."

And with that bit of advice, she gives me a small, sad wave and walks away. Leaving me standing next to the luggage and a mountain of regret. So I take her advice to try to fix this with Lilly. I pick up my phone and dial her number, hoping she'll give me a chance to explain. No answer. Damn it.

CHAPTER 33

Lilly

I WAKE THE NEXT DAY to Amy snoring next to me and a pounding tear- and wine-induced headache. I look at my phone to see that it's dead, and when I go to charge the battery, I remember my charger is in my suitcase, which is sitting in the trunk of Oliver's car. And then the memories of the last twenty-four hours come pouring back in, along with another barrage of tears. With the knowledge that there's no way I can face a day at O'Brien/O'Ryan Real Estate today, I use Amy's phone to call in sick and sink back under the covers and into unconscious bliss.

When I wake up again a couple of hours later, I see a note from Amy telling me she had to get home to get ready for her shift at the hospital and that she loves me and she'll call me later. Thanks to my sick day, I now have the day to myself, so I lie back down in bed and think about what Amy said to me last night. Did I blow everything out of proportion? Do I owe Oliver the chance to tell his side of the story? While I ponder this, not sure what is reality and what is the product of my own insecurities, there's a knock at the door. That's weird. No one other than Amy ever visits me. As I run a hand over my hair to tame it into a presentable form, I wobble to the front door and look out the peephole. Oliver. Just standing there looking as delectable as he always does. What's he doing here? Why isn't he at work?

As I open the door, just a little bit, I poke my head out and get a better look at him. He's gorgeous, as always, but also tired and a bit rumpled. Very unlike the normal, always neat man I know and love.

"Can I come in?" he asks. I take a moment to stare at his ruffled hair and his tired eyes and finally stand aside, opening the door wider to let him in. Oliver gives me a grateful half smile and enters the apartment, wheeling in my suitcase behind him.

"I thought you would need this." He gestures to the suitcase at his feet.

Still not saying anything, I grab the case and walk it into my room, giving myself the chance to find some equilibrium. I muster up the strength to face him and find out what he has to say to me and walk back to where I left him.

After clearing his throat, Oliver starts, "Amy mentioned you called in sick today. That's why I knew you were here."

I nod and walk into my small kitchen, knowing I need coffee to get through whatever this conversation will be.

"We need to talk," Oliver says from right behind me, so close I can feel the heat of his body against my back. I take a deliberate step away from him, offering him a coffee, and get to work making two cups, happy to have something to keep my hands occupied.

"Lilly, can you stop and look at me?"

I know I'm behaving childishly but can't stop myself, so I continue to ignore his presence and delay what I believe will be the inevitable "let's just stay friends" conversation.

"Lilly, I'm sorry," he says finally.

At this, I stop and look at him. Really look at him. At this man I love so much it hurts. His deep-brown eyes have dark circles under them, like he, too, had a restless night, and his beautiful lips are turned down into a sad frown. He's hurting, and I want to help make it better for him, so I tell him what I think he wants to hear.

"It's OK, Ol. I know we were just pretending this past weekend. You have nothing to be sorry about."

Oliver looks like I've just sucker punched him, and after taking a breath, he goes to speak. I interrupt him before he can say anything further.

"You obviously have some unresolved feelings for Emma, which is natural given you just broke up, and I don't want to hurt your relationship. I don't want to be the reason you're ever unhappy."

"But, Lilly, you've got it all wrong," he says, cutting me off in an attempt to stem the flow of my rambling.

"I don't think so," I tell him with fake confidence. "You should be with Emma. You guys are perfect for each other. And me? Well, I'm always one minute away from disaster. Why would you want to deal with that on a regular basis?" I turn away so he won't see my eyes fill with tears and pick up my cup, walking into the other room.

Oliver follows again, close behind me. "You don't mean that, do you?"

"Sure I do," I tell him in a voice that breaks halfway through. "You're the best person I know, and you deserve the best."

"But, Lilly," he says only for me to cut him off again.

"Ollie, you don't need to make excuses or lie to make me feel better. It's OK."

Oliver opens his mouth to argue with me, and I shut it down again. I need for him to leave so I can fall apart in peace.

"Oliver, I need you to go now. As much as I always love having you around, right now you're the last person I want to see." I look at him, pleading for him to understand that he cannot make this better, that at this moment, he's making me hurt too much.

Oliver must see the pain written on my face, as he takes a step towards me, stopping when he sees me retreat from him. He swallows hard, standing there for a moment, looking so lost that I almost give in and beg for him to "pick me, choose me, love me" à la Meredith Grey to Derek Shepherd. Before I can do any of this, he turns and walks to the door.

"Just so you know, this past weekend was not pretending for me," he says, his back to me as he opens the door.

I can't understand why he's saying this to me now. When we had the chance to spend the evening together yesterday, to talk about our relationship, and he instead chose to go and speak to Emma. Surely that meant he wanted to work things out with her? I didn't get this all wrong, did I? Feeling flustered and confused by my tumultuous thoughts, I say the first thing that comes to my mind. "I think it's best we spend some time apart. I need some space to figure this all out."

Oliver pauses in the act of opening the front door and turns to me. "If that's what you want, Lilly, then I'll give you space. I'll give you anything you want." And with that, he walks out of the apartment, closing the door softly behind him. And I sink to the floor and cry, more confused and heartbroken than ever.

After peeling myself off the floor some twenty minutes and a bucket of tears later, I grab my phone charger and set about getting my phone in working order. Once my phone has been charged, I send Amy an essay text message outlining my encounter with Oliver and the emotional damage it inflicted on me. Amy sends back a crying face emoji, letting me know she's too busy at work to deal with my trauma. At this, I throw my phone back on my bed and head to the bathroom to shower off the ickiness of the past few hours.

In the shower, while I shampoo and condition my hair several times, I reflect on everything Oliver has said and done over the past weekend, starting with agreeing to be my fake boyfriend in the first place, through to the many public displays of affection, culminating in the mind-blowing kisses. He says it was all real, but if that is the case, why did he leave me to go to Emma? Why, at the first chance to prove how he feels for me, did he let me down like that? And then there's the idea that maybe I'm blowing what Oliver did out of proportion. Could Amy be right? Was I being too quick to believe the worst in Oliver, instead of allowing him to be human and make mistakes? Maybe he regretted what happened yesterday and that's why he came here, to clear things up? But could it really be that simple? He was with Emma for almost a year; there must have been something real between them, more real than our weekend of make believe. And Emma is perfect for him. I will do well not to forget that little fact.

With the water running cold and no closer to understanding anything, I turn off the tap and dry myself. Dressing in my softest, most comfortable sweatshirt and pants, I towel off my hair and leave it to air dry. As I catch sight of my now legendary New Year's resolution to-do list, sitting on my coffee table mocking me, there's a sense of sadness as I focus on number four on the list. The idea of getting over Oliver feels like a lost cause after having a taste of what being with him feels like.

With the chances of ticking off numbers one and two in my sight, I put thoughts of my doomed love life aside and do some work on my Love, Lilly Instagram page, which has been neglected over the past several days. I add a photo of myself taken by Oliver on the weekend, glammed up in the Perfect Dress and caption it, "Lilly in Love (with this dress)," which in no time at all gains a thousand likes and as many comments, and decide in that moment to do an Instagram Live video later this afternoon, to distract myself from the train wreck that is my love life. I plan to do a Love, Lilly lesson: how to bake, breakup edition. It seems like perfect timing to me, given that Valentine's Day has just passed and there may be a few lonely hearts out there waiting to connect with mine. I spend some time looking through my recipe cards before finding the perfect treat to feature in this segment, breakup brownies, which are just brownies that are easy to make in any state of emotional turmoil.

After gathering my ingredients, I attempt to get myself camera ready, which involves some concealer on my under-eye circles (which match the ones Oliver was sporting), some blush to take away the unnatural pallor of my tear-soaked skin, and some lip gloss for confidence. I start my Instagram Live by telling the viewers the purpose of today's session:

"Hi, friends. Today I'm going to show you how to make breakup brownies, which are like my normal brownies but with double the amount of chocolate chips to help take away the pain of love gone wrong. I know we just had the holiday to celebrate love, aka Valentine's Day, but if there are any people like me out there, feeling unlovable today, know that you're not alone!"

I continue my lesson by outlining how to bring together all the ingredients while staring at my screen and reading the many comments flying in from the viewers. Many are concerned, wanting to know if I broke up with "the hottie from the photo," with others saying, "Why do you look so sad?" and, "We love you, Lilly!" I keep up a running commentary while I assemble the ingredients, talking to my viewers about heartache.

"It's like on Grey's Anatomy, you know? When Derek 'McDreamy' Shepherd leaves Meredith to go back to his wife, the perfect Addison Montgomery-Shepherd." I stop to wipe a tear away. Thinking about that episode in my current emotional state is a recipe for disaster. "And then Meredith has to continue seeing him at work while knowing that he didn't love her enough to pick her. It was brutal. And given that she was a surgical intern then, she didn't have the time to bake breakup brownies, but I think she should have," I continue, putting the brownies in the oven to bake. "Because in a mere twenty-five minutes, when these come out of the oven, all warm and gooey, they're going to be the cure for any pain you're feeling."

As all the positive comments and emojis pour in, I feel a teensy bit better from the outpouring of Internet love, and once I've completed the recipe, I tell my viewers I will post a picture of the final product once baked and sign off for the evening. After I end the video, glowing a little from the success of it all, I make the mistake of looking at the last picture I posted on my Instagram feed and see that Oliver has commented, "Perfect dress on the perfect girl." Oh, Ollie, what are you doing to me?

CHAPTER 34

Oliver

As I leave Lilly's apartment, I'm tempted to do the sad guy stroll, wandering the streets, feeling sorry for myself, you know, like they do in the movies. Except in the movies, it's always raining for the heartbroken man, and just my luck. Today is a sunny day. Also, looking around this neighbourhood, I'm not sure I or my wallet would make it back in one piece. Lilly really needs to move. So instead, I get in my car and settle in for a long, miserable drive, listening to sad music and lamenting every misstep I've taken in the last twenty-four hours. How am I here? Yesterday morning, I woke up beside the woman I've loved for almost a decade, and we were on our way to being something together, something real. And now we're here, with me behaving like a lovesick fool.

When I woke up this morning, after a restless night of alternating between trying to sleep and trying to call Lilly (still no response), I finally got a few text messages from Amy. The first one cussed me out for being an idiot, well deserved. The second one took pity on me and told me Lilly's phone battery was dead because someone had her charger (me). And the last one informed me that Lilly called in sick and would be home all day. Thank you, Amy! Now I had an excuse to see her and beg for her forgiveness. Without a second thought, I called in to work and took a personal day, unheard of for me, highlighting how out of character I've been behaving of late, and then I rushed to Lilly's place. I thought I could fix it. Just explain to her what happened with Emma (not that I fully understand it all myself) and confess my undying love for her. Too much? Perhaps. But I was a desperate man.

When I saw Lilly, with her sad, teary eyes and red nose, I wanted to kick myself. Hard. I did that. I made her cry. And for what? An attempt to keep the peace and be the good guy? I was hoping for just a couple of minutes to explain my actions and was blindsided when Lilly refused to hear me, refused to even look at me. And then she gave me the knockout blow: "It's OK, Ol. I know we were just pretending this past weekend." I don't know where Lilly's head is at. Does she really believe that after the weekend we spent together, that I'd just skip back into my relationship with Emma? Was I not clear about the way I was feeling about her? Did she think I was just pretending? Was she just pretending?

With these thoughts swirling around my mind—could it be true, could Lilly have just been caught up in the moment and was trying to let me down gently?—I drive past the local bar and decide to embrace this new, reckless side of my character and park in front. A beer or two at lunchtime sounds like the ticket to getting through this day. I pull up a bar stool and order a local brew, waiting impatiently for the numbing effects of alcohol to kick in. Unfortunately, luck isn't on my side today (first the sunshine and now the propensity to remain sober), and it takes more than several beers and several hours to feel OK again. As I hear my phone ping, I dive for it. Lilly? No, just Dale. Dale, the traitor who tried to flirt with Lilly. Do I like Dale?

DALE: Hey, bud. I heard you're off sick today, are you OK?

OLIVER: Nope.

DALE: What happened? Where are you?

OLIVER: Lilly happened. Drinking now.

DALE: Where exactly are you drinking? I'll come and get you.

Maybe Dale isn't so bad. I text him the address, my bleary eyes making this task take longer than necessary, then sit back again and order another beer.

Twenty minutes later, Dale walks in. Dressed for work. Work, where I should have been today. Where I need to be to get ahead in life. Where I would have been if I hadn't made a mess of everything. Boy, I'm a depressing drunk.

"Hey, dude, are you OK?"

"Sure, never better," I slur back. I'm not OK.

"What happened? Last I heard, you and Lilly were off for a romantic weekend of fake dating."

I groan as I put my head on the table and tell him everything. Dale, being a good friend, orders a beer and sits back to listen to the whole sordid tale.

"And then she asked for some space, and I know I should respect that, but I just want to call her and beg her to listen...," I finish up.

"Man, that's quite the story. I can understand why you're here, day drinking. But I don't think all is lost. Sounds like you've hurt Lilly and she needs a minute to lick her wounds. Give her the space she needs and then try again." Dale is wise. He's like Yoda.

"You think?" I ask, desperate for some hope. "OK, I'll give her a few days, and then I'll fight for her."

Dale nods, and I feel buoyed again. I will make this work; I will get Lilly back.

"C'mon, Ol. I'll take you home. You're in no state to drive."

As I get into the passenger seat of Dale's car, I pull out my phone and see the latest photo posted on the Love, Lilly Instagram page. Lilly in that dress—it almost hurts to look at her.

"Perfect dress on the perfect girl," I comment before I can stop myself. Because she's the perfect girl for me, and as I continue to look at her, I declare to myself that sooner or later, she will be mine.

CHAPTER 35

Lilly

T HE NEXT DAY, MUCH TO my dismay, I have to drag myself to work, having used all my allocated sick leave the day before. I know I must look dreadful, as my work colleagues appear to be giving me a wide berth while asking if I'm still contagious, and I set my mind to the mindless tasks in front of me. The monotonous routine of the day, in addition to all the work I have to catch up on from yesterday, means that the day passes by quickly. During my breaks, I work on my Instagram account, posting some sponsored ads and playing with the filters for some of my upcoming pictures. My pop-up café is opening in three weeks, and I know I need to focus on getting ready for that, but my heart is just not in it. And to add insult to injury, this weekend is my twenty-fourth birthday. Another year older, and not even a little bit wiser.

After I return home following a day of endless paperwork, I call Amy to see if she can shed any light on my current dire love life situation. Amy, true to form, is still encouraging me to hear Oliver out, believing that maybe I was too hasty in sending him away. Oliver has been silent. Apart from that comment on Instagram, I haven't heard from him at all. In typical Oliver fashion, he's honouring my request for space. And in my own typical fashion, I'm annoyed that I had been so hasty in sending him away and am hoping he will ignore my wishes and turn back up on my doorstep, ready to explain what happened. Maybe this time, I'll be in the right head space to actually listen.

At home and feeling restless, I begin making myself dinner, comfort mac 'n' cheese tonight, when my phone rings. My heart in my throat, thinking maybe it's Oliver, I grab it up from the bench. In place of where Oliver's face should be are my parents', attempting to FaceTime me upside down.

"Hi, Mum. Hi, Dad. You have to turn the phone the other way around," I say to them as I answer. I hear grumbling and see them finally turn themselves the right way up.

"Hi, Lilly. Honey, how are you?" my mum asks, looking concerned.

"I'm OK, Mum. Just had a long day at work and am now making myself some dinner."

"Are you sure you're OK?" my dad chimes in from where his head is pressed close to Mum's on the screen.

"Ummm, yes?" I say, feeling confused by their concern.

"We watched your video last night. On the Instagram," my mum informs me, sounding very much like someone who doesn't know how to use "the" Instagram. "You looked so sad, and you were making breakup brownies."

"You watched my video?" I ask, dumbfounded.

"Of course. We've subscribed to your page and get a little notification when you're starting a live video," my dad informs me. "We loved the one where you made mini chocolate mint ice cream sandwiches. Your mother tried to make them for me. However, they did not work out well."

As they laugh together, my mum tells me, "I don't have your skills in the kitchen, Lilly," shocking me further. "But I love the way you explain the baking process, so I've been saving each video post and am trying to improve each time I make something you suggest."

I stare at my parents while they continue to talk about which recipe they want to try next and can't process what I'm hearing.

"Are you telling me you've been following me on Instagram?" I ask, trying to get some clarity.

"Yes, Lilly. After you told us your plans to work on Instagram" —I roll my eyes at their description of being an influencer as someone who "works on Instagram," like it's in an office somewhere— "we did some research and found that it's a legitimate way to make an income if done correctly. So we started following you. Haven't you noticed our comments?"

"No," I tell them. "You've been commenting on my posts?"

"Every one of them," my dad says. "We have the username @Mum_and_Dad. Lilly, after we saw how much you seemed to be enjoying your work, we've been following along closely. And we just love what you're doing."

I feel bewildered as I take in what they're saying to me. "You're proud of what I'm doing?"

"Yes, of course we are," my mum says. "Your page is delightful. Filled with lovely recipes and fun photos. And all your witty commentary in your live videos, well, we find it hilarious. And as we said, our research showed us that you can make a lot of money on Instagram, and while it's not a long-term prospect, you can make the sort of money that will set you up for your café business."

"I can't believe you've been doing research into Instagram earning potential," I say, unable to comprehend what they're telling me.

"Not just Instagram, but the TikTok as well," my dad chimes in, rendering me mute with shock. "Not everyone can be successful in this space. In fact, our research says that most aren't, but, Lilly, your accounts have hundreds of thousands of followers. It's very impressive."

Huh. Is this what it feels like to have my parents be proud of me? So unfamiliar to me.

"I didn't think you'd be interested in any of this. In fact, I thought you'd talk me out of it. The last time we spoke, you were encouraging me to look into internships at a finance institute," I reminded them.

My parents have the grace to look embarrassed by this.

"We know we have seemed dismissive of some of your plans in the past, Lilly. And we shouldn't have been. It's just been so hard watching you flounder since leaving university, and we thought by suggesting some career options, we were being helpful."

"But we realise you didn't need that from us," my mum continues. "That you already had a path you were forging and that all we needed to do was support you on your way."

Tears fill my eyes as I listen to what my parents are telling me. "So you aren't disappointed in me? That I didn't follow in your footsteps and do something more academically inclined?"

At this, it's my parents' turn to look shocked.

"Is that what you thought? That we were disappointed in you?" my mum asks.

"Well, yes," I tell them. "You were always pushing me away from my dreams, towards your own. I guess I never felt like I was good enough for you." In saying this, I feel a sense of relief that it's out in the open.

"Lilly, you listen to me," my mum says, staring at me from the screen. "Not for one moment, not one minute in your life, have you ever been a disappointment to us. And we're sorry if we made you feel that way," she finishes, her eyes now filled with tears.

"You're our greatest gift, Lil," my father continues, his voice gruff with emotion. "Our greatest achievement, and we are proud of you and the life you have made for yourself every single day. You're so fearless, and you will do such great things with your life. And we are proud to watch you succeed in whatever way you want your life to go."

I feel a weight lift from my chest at hearing the words from my parents that I've wanted to hear my whole life, and I give them a watery smile.

"Really?" I ask, needing further reinforcement.

My parents smile at me, their eyes still wet with tears. "Yes, Lilly. And we're sorry if we ever made you doubt this."

I grin at my parents now, feeling like we're finally on the same page. "So which one of my posts is your favourite?"

As they laugh, they each tell me which post they loved the most, and why, arguing between themselves. As I watch on, my heart fills with joy at this moment. After we chat for a while longer, with my parents promising to come down and visit the weekend of my pop-up café, I say goodbye to them and hang up, feeling a bit dazed.

I think back now to what I discussed with Amy, how I have felt unwanted and unloved by my own parents, and I wonder how I got it all so wrong. Granted, my parents had never been effusive in their approval of me, as they were today, but they've always supported me. And while they often tried to steer me in directions that made sense to them, my mum was the one who encouraged me to take up baking as a hobby when I first spoke about it with them, and she even subscribed to a few cooking magazines to help guide me on my way. They may never have agreed outright with this as a career path, but they never stood in my way either. I was looking at our relationship through the lens of my own insecurities and got it all so wrong.

I pick up the phone to call Amy, hoping she's available for another therapy session. When she answers and clarifies that she has some free time, I unload on her everything that happened in the past thirty minutes.

"Lilly," Amy says, when I've finished my monologue, "I've always known your parents love and support you. You were too busy feeling down on yourself to believe this. And for the past year, you have been floating along, a little bit aimlessly, until you started working on your New Year's resolution list. It's given you a purpose, and I've noticed a big change in you over the past month. You're more confident and more driven. And you're now in a place to receive this support from your parents."

"Wow, you sound like Oprah," I tell her, laughing a little through more tears. "You're right. I know you're right. I was feeling so negative about my life that I was projecting it onto how I saw others viewing me. My parents didn't deserve that."

"Not just your parents," Amy says, not being subtle.

"You mean Oliver?" I ask. "You think I've been projecting the same way onto him?"

"I don't know for sure, Lil. But I think it's worth thinking about. If you don't feel you deserve love, then you won't be able to receive it either."

Amy's words cut through me like a knife, which is what she intended. Was I running away from Oliver before he had the chance to walk away from me? Is it a case of feeling unlovable so I leave before he can see me that way too?

"I have a lot to think about," I tell Amy, already pondering which cookies I'll bake while I do this.

"You know I'm here as a sounding board if you need," Amy offers. "And bake an extra batch of whatever you settle on for me," she adds, reading my mind and knowing me a little too well.

"And think about what you want to do for your birthday this weekend, because I'm not letting you celebrate another year of life in some sad, miserable, alone state," she adds to lighten the mood.

I laugh at her description of the mess I was in last year and how I'm not too far off from that state this year and agree to think about it. Add it to the whole list of thinking I have in store for this evening.

"Love you, Lilly," Amy says, signing off.

"Thanks, Ames. Love you too."

I get to work in the kitchen, focusing on the tasks of making cookies and learning to love myself. Boy, do I have quite the evening ahead.

CHAPTER 36

Oliver

AMY: *Enough giving Lilly space.*

AMY: *You need to do something.*

AMY: *The girls and I are taking Lilly out for her birthday. Joe's Bar at 7:30 p.m.*

AMY: *Bring your A game!*

OLIVER: *Thank you, little sis. I owe you one.*

CHAPTER 37

Lilly

THE NEXT FEW DAYS PASS by in a blur of breakdowns and break-throughs. After my conversation with my parents and my debrief with Amy, I'm beginning to see my past behaviour differently. I see a pattern of always presenting my life choices to my parents in a negative light, expecting them to react in a certain way and almost manifesting the result. I see also how in the past, I started my relationships with men filled with my own insecurities, always thinking the worst was going to happen, to be prepared for when it eventually did.

I think back specifically on my time with Sebastian. We were friends first, so I approached this relationship a little differently, but all the same tendencies appeared nonetheless. I started the relationship by being the "perfect" girlfriend, and then over time, I let my true self show. When that happened and he rejected me, I rationalised it was my actual personality that was the turn off. Now I realise all those guys had started dating a fake version of me, so of course they broke up with me once I changed. I had been misrepresenting myself from the beginning—am I like Grant 2.0?—always setting myself up for failure.

And that's why I've been struggling so much with what happened with Oliver. He knew me, the real me, so I struggled to believe he could ever fall for me. Even after spending that weekend with him where I could see the obvious affection he has for me, and with people around me telling me he cares for me, my insecurities would not let me believe that perhaps, one day, he could love me. And when he walked away from me, rejected me for someone I perceive as better than me, it was like picking at a scab on an old wound. It hurt. It reinforced the idea I have that I'm less than or unworthy. So instead of hearing him out and letting him explain, I walked away. I left him before we were even anything real, before he could properly leave me. I let the fear that I'm ultimately not enough drive me away from the one person who has always made me feel like more than enough.

And now, after all this soul searching, Amy is still insisting we go out tonight to celebrate my birthday. The big twenty-four. With things such a mess with Oliver, I can't conceive of getting dressed up and being among people, but when Amy has her mind set on something, it's impossible to get her to budge. Like right now—she has just finished fixing my hair into relaxed waves and already has an outfit ready to go on my bed.

"Can we just cancel and have Madi and Sammi meet us here? We can stay in and watch a movie?" I ask, for the hundredth time, while she's applying my eyeliner to make my eyes look cat-like.

"No! You will not be a sad lady at home on your birthday. Not on my watch. We're going out because we are all young and we are all hot."

"OK, OK," I tell her in surrender. "Just don't let me drink too much. I'm turning over a new leaf and vowing to make fewer stupid decisions in my twenty-fourth year of life."

Amy laughs as she works on the next eye. "I can't make any promises."

After I force myself into some skinny jeans and a slinky top and shove my feet into a pair of heels, we make our way out to the new trendiest bar in town. We meet Madi and Sammi out front and skip the line, thanks to some VIP connections Amy made with some high-profile patient she had looked after in the emergency room last week, apparently. Once inside, we find ourselves a table and order a drink.

"To my best friend, on your birthday. I love you like a sister! Have an amazing birthday," Amy toasts when we get our drinks. Madi and Sammi cheer, and I smile at their antics, taking small sips of my drink and looking around. The bar is full of good-looking men, but my eyes keep searching for one man in particular.

"How are you doing?" Madi asks me with some concern. I have brought both Madi and Sammi up to speed on everything from the wedding weekend and beyond, with many video chats taking place this past week. And while they've given me their full support, I know on the inside they're both team "Lilliver."

"I'm OK," I tell them. When they all look at me, unconvinced, I finally break down and ask Amy, "How's Oliver doing?" I was holding off on trying to extract information from her, not wanting to put her in the awkward position of being in the middle.

"He's OK," Amy replies, not giving much away.

"He hasn't contacted me for my birthday," I tell her, feeling a little pitiful as I say it and as Sammi rubs my arm to comfort me.

"You told him you needed space, and that boy is very good at following instructions," Amy points out, ever the voice of reason.

I nod and feel sad that this is the case. "I know. I just wish he would fight for me a little. If he wants me, that is. Maybe he has just given up and is with Emma now?" I look at Amy, hoping to get a hint as to whether this is true. Amy has mentioned nothing about Emma since that fateful night when Oliver chose Emma over me, and I'm desperate for any information as to where I may stand.

Amy waves her hand in a dismissive gesture. "Enough about boys. We are four strong, independent women. All our conversations don't need to revolve around men." When the three of us give her a doubtful look, she continues, "Let's talk about your pop-up café and the plans you have in place." With this, I let myself get distracted from thoughts of Oliver and Emma. I tell my friends about what I have planned to bake for the inaugural café session, wanting their opinions on whether I'm on the right track.

After an hour and two drinks, though the conversation has been lively and fun, I'm ready to go. My friends have tried their best to make this a fun evening for me, with Madi offering to get phone numbers from the cute guys around us and Sammi attempting to coax a few laughs out of me, but my heart isn't in it. In fact, my heart is hurting a bit too much to be here. As I tell the girls that I'm ready to call it a night and go home, I hear the music tempo change from the thumping base of whatever latest pop tune is playing to the crooning first notes of Ed Sheeran's "Perfect." I groan at the irony of this song playing at this moment and bend down to pick up my bag, needing to get out of here. As I look up, the crowd parts, and Oliver is standing there. And he's smiling his dimple smile at me. I look at him and then at my friends, who are all smiling at me, giving me encouraging looks, and I slowly stand up and walk towards him.

"You did this? You asked them to play this song? For me?" I ask, astonished that he's here. I stare up at him, my heart racing, wondering if this is his grand gesture. Like in the rom coms I love to watch, where the hero does something romantic to win back the heart of the girl he loves. Could this be what is happening here? My skin tingles in anticipation of what's to come, and I lean towards him, desperate to get close to him after what has felt like a very long week apart.

"It seems appropriate," he says, confirming my suspicions. He asked them to play it for me. I smile at him as he takes my hand, leading me to the dance floor. "It feels like our song."

I nod, because that's how I think of it too, stepping into his arms with a sense of peace settling over me.

"I've missed you this week," Oliver shocks me by saying.

My head shoots up at this, and I stop moving to the music to look at him. "You have?"

"Of course. I always miss you when you're not around, but after being with you last weekend, I've missed you like crazy."

I stare at Oliver, speechless, and begin moving to the music again, stepping closer into his arms.

"Lilly, I'm so sorry about the way I behaved last Sunday. You did not deserve it."

I resist the urge to tell him it's OK and wipe the slate clean, asking instead, "What happened? Why did you go to her like that?"

"I don't know, Lil. I guess I felt bad?"

He takes a deep breath after I nod for him to go on. "Emma has always been funny about you. For our entire relationship, she hinted at me having feelings for you. And she was right, of course," he says, shocking me some more. "So, when I saw her, I didn't want to hurt her with the reality that she had been right and that the minute we broke up, I finally acted on the feelings I've had for you for so long. And I guess I sort of had a moment of confusion. I've wanted to be with you for so long that the reality of it felt so momentous. What if I messed things up and we ruined our friendship? What if you decided I'm too boring and ordinary for you? All these thoughts have been playing in my mind, so in that split second, I made a stupid decision, and I hurt you. And I'm so sorry for that, Lil."

At this confession, feeling breathless, I move in even closer and focus on the only part of his declaration that is reverberating in my mind. "You have feelings for me?"

Oliver looks at me in dismay. "I'm so in love with you. I've been in love with you for as long as I can remember. I told you last weekend that I wish you could see yourself the way I see you. Lilly, you light up every room you enter. You're spontaneous and crazy. You fill every space with laughter and fun. You're so beautiful, even with mascara running down your face." He says this part with a smile as I laugh at the memory. "You have been the best part of every memory I have, and I adore every single part of you. Even the parts that don't seem to know how to arrive anywhere on time." I laugh at this joke and soak in everything he has said to me. Oliver sees me, the good parts and the bad, and he loves them all. What more could I ask for?

With this thought in my mind, I'm unable to resist him any longer. I launch myself at him, kissing him with abandon. The kiss goes on and on until finally, Oliver lifts his head and asks almost timidly, "Does that mean you have feelings for me too?"

I grin at him, feeling so happy my cheeks hurt from smiling so big. "Of course I have feelings for you. I'm so in love with you I can barely see straight. Oliver, you have been my hero and my pro-tector for as long as I can remember. You're the highlight of my childhood, and as an adult, I know I can't live without you. And it's not just because you're good with the organising and stuff," I say with a big smile, wanting to tease him just a little bit. Oliver laughs with me, and I squeal in delight as he picks me up and spins me around.

"You love me?" he asks again.

"I do. So much. You're my Derek Shepherd," I tell him, ignoring the confused look on his face. "You're my person. And I think that maybe we are perfect for each other."

At this, he grabs my face and kisses me again. The kiss grows in urgency, turning into something more, and when we finally come up for air, Oliver says again with complete sincerity, "I'm so sorry I hurt you like that, Lil. I will regret it forever. I hope I can make it up to you."

I hug him tightly, knowing that what he did came from a place of both insecurity and decency, and forgive him in an instant.

"It's OK, Ol. I understand now." Smiling up at him, I probe for more details. "So when did you know you were in love with me?"

Oliver laughs and pulls me closer again. "You want all the details, hey?"

"Every one of them!" I demand, filled with delirious happiness.

"I seem to recall it was an ordinary afternoon, when you had been dumped by that jerk Zack Petty. And I just looked at you and I knew. And I haven't been able to shake the feeling ever since."

I feel breathless again at this confession. I remember that day so clearly. And that means he has loved me since he was eighteen. Feeling generous in the face of such vulnerability, I tell him, "I've been in love with you since before then, but true to form, I was a little late in realising it. But I know now that you have always been it for me," I disclose, earning myself another heated kiss, one that makes my toes tingle and my heart do a happy dance.

Once I'm able to come up for air, we look over to where my friends are standing, grinning at us, Amy with Dr Lucas McHottie standing close behind her—interesting—and I blow them a kiss. I turn back to Oliver and kiss him again, revelling in the fact that I can now do this whenever I want. Oliver, groaning, kisses me back, equally happy that our pretending days are over. We kiss again for so long that my friends have to interrupt us, to tell us they're leaving and to wish me the happiest of birthdays.

I hug them each goodbye, holding on to Amy for a little longer, telling her in a soft voice, "Thank you, Ames. For always believing in me, even when I didn't believe in myself. And for pushing me into wanting more for myself. I love you!"

Amy looks at me with tears in her eyes, smiling at me. "Lilly, you deserve the world. I'm so pleased you got your happy ending."

And then she turns to Oliver and says in a stern voice, "Don't mess this up!"

Oliver laughs and nods and pulls me back into his arms. Together we watch my friends leave, with Amy walking out with Lucas—I need to find out what's going on there—and we walk off the dance floor together.

"Do you want to go somewhere quiet and talk some more?" Oliver asks, close to my ear.

I think about the fact that it's my birthday and there has been no cake and exclaim, "Let's get some dessert!"

Oliver nods and, taking my hand, leads me out of the club. As we're walking, I ask him one last time, just to be sure, "You really love me?"

Oliver stops, brushes his lips over mine, and looking deep into my eyes, tells me, "Yes, Lilly Hamilton. I really love you. To me, you are perfect."

At this I give him a big smile and take his hand, happy that we are finally on the same page. As we leave, I think back to my now infamous New Year's resolution to-do list and, in my mind, cross off number four. Resolution sorted. I can now add to any to-do list moving forward, love Oliver and only Oliver from now until forever.

The End.

EPILOGUE

Oliver

Twelve months later...

T ODAY IS THE GRAND OPENING of the Love, Lilly café. I watch with pride as Lilly works the room, charming everyone she meets, and I take in all that she has achieved. Here, today, she's surrounded by family and friends, everyone who loves her, and she's confident in who she is, soaking in the praise and adoration from everyone around her. Lilly has changed so much from that girl I picked up stranded on the side of the road just over one year ago.

As I watch her, I think back over the past year that I've been lucky enough to call her mine. The first few weeks of dating Lilly were as close to bliss as possible. We spent every spare moment together; Amy told us we were nauseatingly inseparable. My bosses at work were not thrilled when they noticed I was spending fewer hours at the office in the evenings and on the weekends, and as a result, my much-sought-after promotion went to someone else. And I couldn't find it in me to care. After spending so much of my adult life working towards something more, it felt good to enjoy my life in the here and now.

And enjoying it I have been. After the first month of being with Lilly, with her spending every night at my house, I convinced her to leave her apartment and move in with me. Lilly, Amy and I were all thrilled with this decision, Johnny not so much. Amy was especially happy with this move, as she had her best friend and an expert baker as her roommate.

A month after Lilly moved in, my parents decided to sell our family home and split the profits between me and Amy, to buy ourselves somewhere to call our own. Lilly and I, after much deliberation and many open-house inspections (because we needed to find a place with the perfect kitchen, you see), found a cute two-bedroom town house with a small yard, close to where Amy purchased her own place. Lilly has loved attempting (unsuccessfully) to grow a veggie garden, and she's now begging me to get a rescue puppy. So far, I've held firm in my decision to not get one, but as is the case with Lilly, she and I both know she'll get her way eventually.

Over these past few months, Lilly has also been working hard to turn this Love, Lilly vision into a reality. Her inaugural pop-up café was a roaring success. Because of her popularity on social media, hundreds of people attended the first session, causing her to run out of food to serve by lunchtime. By using the income from the weekly pop-up café and the money she was making from sponsorship deals on Instagram and TikTok, about six months ago, Lilly resigned from that awful real estate office, and from then had been focusing on opening a full-time brick-and-mortar Love, Lilly café and bakery. In true Lilly form, when she went in to quit her job, she did so in style, telling her awful bosses where they could shove their job while also leaving behind a platter of cookies for them to enjoy.

And as for me, I've been spending every day feeling forever grateful that I can now call her mine. A few days ago, she found her old New Year's resolution to-do list and with a laugh showed me item number four—where she had replaced "get over little Oliver crush" with "stay in love with Oliver forever." And so it seems fitting, that here, today, on Valentine's Day, I make this a reality. I nervously pat the engagement ring in my pocket and hope she will say yes. And that I will be lucky enough to spend the rest of my life loving Lilly.

If you enjoyed Love, Lilly, it would mean the world to me if you could leave a review or a rating on a site like Goodreads, Amazon or wherever you purchased this book.

Reviews mean so much to authors and could very well be the motivation needed to keep writing, and to publish that next novel.

Also, if want to read a little bit more of Lilly and Oliver you can get a free bonus chapter by going to my website and signing up to my newsletter.

Amy and Lucas's story, Always, Amy is available June 2023. Read on for an expert from chapter one.

ALWAYS, AMY

Amy

I WATCH MY BIG BROTHER get down on one knee and propose to my very choked-up, deliriously happy best friend, and smile. I could not be any happier for the two of them. They finally got over themselves and chose happiness together. As Lilly bursts into tears, also getting down on her knees to accept the proposal, squealing, "Yes!" I jump up and down in delight. They are such a good match. Oliver is the perfect balm for Lilly's particular brand of crazy, and Oliver is a lighter, happier version of himself when Lilly is around.

Once they have finished kissing, I grab two glasses of champagne and head over to them.

"Congratulations, my sister-in-law-to-be!" I yell, grabbing Lilly in a full-body bear hug.

With tears streaming down her face, Lilly hugs me back, whispering, "I'm so happy," in a soft voice.

Oliver joins us in the hug, and the three of us do a little happy dance shuffle.

"You did good, big bro." I look at the giant rock of an engagement ring he has just put on to Lilly's finger. It's an oval cut, about seventeen carats from the looks of it, on a slim yellow-gold band. It is beautiful. And I can tell that Lilly thinks so too. As she waves it in front of our faces, we both marvel at how sparkly it is.

"Now you will officially be part of the family," I tell Lilly, who knows she has always been an honorary Harlow. As Lilly grins at the thought, both Lilly's parents and mine interrupt our conversation, all four of them wanting a piece of the future bride and groom.

I step back to give them some space and look around the room. Spying a sample tray of brownies, I chase after the waitress, hoping to get one before they disappear. Lilly's baking business has expanded rapidly over the past six months, and with it, her baking prowess has grown tenfold. Everything Lilly makes is next-level delicious. I manage to capture not one but two treats for myself and head to a corner to enjoy them in solitude. After taking my first bite—oh, Lilly, these are so good they should be illegal—I scan the room, ecstatic at the large turnout for this special occasion.

When I see Dale across the room, flirting with our friend Sammi, I smile at him and nod and continue my perusal. And then I see him. Him. No, that can't be right. He isn't even in the country. Last I heard, he was still in Florence. I rub my eyes to check that my mind isn't playing tricks on me. It is him. Lucas freaking Mancini is here, in the flesh, and he's walking towards me. I'm not ready.

To avoid eye contact and to delay this inevitable meeting, I look towards the exit with desperation. Which is directly behind him. I look around, frantic now, and try to think of a way to make myself invisible—

"Amy," comes his deep voice right in front of me.

I steel my spine, knowing that any chance to escape is long gone, and look up at him. And look up and up some more. In the twelve months he has been gone, I forgot how tall he is. And how mouth-wateringly good looking he is. With his deep-blue eyes and his stupid chiselled jaw. He's like one of Lilly's desserts, so good he should be illegal.

"Lucas," I say, proud that my voice is steady. "What are you doing here?"

"I follow Lilly on Instagram and saw that she's having her grand opening today. I wanted to come and congratulate her, and to see you—"

"When did you get back?"

Lucas gives me a strange look before answering, "I've been back a few weeks. Didn't you get my messages?"

Lucas must be unaware that I blocked his number and muted all his social media accounts the minute he walked out the door all those months ago.

"I must have missed them. I've been pretty busy, you know..." I trail off as Lucas reaches out to touch my arm only to stop when I take a hasty step backwards.

"Anyway, it's good to see you," I lie. "But I must get back to my family. It's a big day for all of us."

Lucas smiles at me, his eyes shadowed with sadness. "I'm so glad those two worked things out." He nods to where Lilly and Oliver are slowly dancing together to no music. "I know how much you wanted them together."

I wince at this, thinking of the night I confided in him, the night of Lilly's birthday when I left the bar with him, right before his abrupt departure. The night I rarely let myself think about any more.

"Yes, they got their happy ending." I start to move away from him now, proud that I got through this conversation without breaking down, and come to a stop when I hear Lucas say from behind me, "I missed you, Amy."

I falter for a moment and only just resist the urge to turn back to him, not wanting to give him the satisfaction of knowing the impact of those words. And with my head held high, I walk away. He doesn't need to know just how much I missed him too.

ACKNOWLEDGEMENTS

THE BIGGEST AND BRIGHTEST THANK you goes to my husband, Philip. Without you, my book would have remained on my laptop, read by no one. Thank you for your enthusiasm for my book and for making this dream of mine a reality. Thank you for being my biggest cheerleader, my emotional support person, my social media manager and everything else in between. My book is out there being read by people solely because of you. I love you so very much. You are my perfect book boyfriend!

To my two beautiful children, Hunter and Sienna. You are the reason for everything I do and I hope every day that I make you proud. I love you both to the moon and back.

To my editor Lyss, thank you for so expertly guiding me through the editing process and helping to make my book come to life. And to my beta readers, you are the reason I didn't give up after that first draft, so thank you!

To my parents, who have always encouraged my love of reading and who have always believed I can do and be anything I put my mind to, thank you! And to my friends and family who have greeted the emergence of this book with so much enthusiasm, I will be forever grateful for the encouragement you have all given me. A special thanks goes to Sarah, for being a delightful disaster and my muse for Lilly.

And finally, to you the reader. By reading this book, you have already made my dreams come true.

Love Always,
Belinda

ABOUT THE AUTHOR

B ELINDA MARY IS A FIRST-time author, but long-time lover of all the books. After studying for ten years and obtaining first a degree in English literature and then a PhD in molecular biology, she has pursued a career in the healthcare industry, and in the last year has taken the leap to fulfil a lifelong dream of writing her debut novel. And when she is not looking after her two kids, her husband of ten years and her crazy spoodle, she can be found on the couch reading, watching all things Bravo, or listening to true crime podcasts.

Belinda hopes to write the kind of stories that she loves to read; filled with laughter, longing and love.

g *@belindamary*   **a** *@belindamary*

⊙ *@belindamary.author*   **f** *@belindamary.author*

www.belindamary.com

www.ingramcontent.com/pod-product-compliance
Lightning Source LLC
Chambersburg PA
CBHW020911130726
47904CB00006BA/1814